## "You saved my life."

Shane wanted to say *And you ruined mine*, and the words were just about to come out of his mouth when he locked eyes with Jess.

Still beautiful. Still haunted. And yet the fixer in him had wanted to fix things for her way back then, and he realized he'd probably do the same thing now.

"All in a day's work," he told her. "You okay?"

"Yes. Thanks to you. Shane, I—"

"Spare me, Jess. I'm not here to walk down memory lane with you or anybody else. There are folks here who need help. A lot of help. I'm here to do a job and happened to run into you along the way."

Her eyes dimmed.

His fault.

But he understood his weakness for her. He'd have scoffed at that notion fifteen minutes ago, but he saw it now, plain as day.

She drew him. She'd done it back then. She did it now. He'd stayed far away purposely, and yet here he was.

Multipublished bestselling author **Ruth Logan Herne**
loves God, her country, her family, dogs, chocolate
and coffee! Married to a very patient man, she lives
in an old farmhouse in Upstate New York and thinks
possums should leave the cat food alone and snakes
should always live outside. There are no exceptions
to either rule! Visit Ruth at ruthloganherne.com.

## Books by Ruth Logan Herne

### Love Inspired

### *Kendrick Creek*

*Rebuilding Her Life*

### *Golden Grove*

*A Hopeful Harvest*
*Learning to Trust*
*Finding Her Christmas Family*

### *Shepherd's Crossing*

*Her Cowboy Reunion*
*A Cowboy in Shepherd's Crossing*
*Healing the Cowboy's Heart*

Visit the Author Profile page
at Harlequin.com for more titles.

# Rebuilding Her Life

## Ruth Logan Herne

LOVE INSPIRED
INSPIRATIONAL ROMANCE

## LOVE INSPIRED®
### INSPIRATIONAL ROMANCE

ISBN-13: 978-1-335-48879-4

Rebuilding Her Life

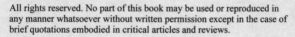

This edition published by arrangement with Harlequin Books S.A.

For questions and comments about the quality of this book, please contact us at CustomerService@Harlequin.com.

Love Inspired
22 Adelaide St. West, 40th Floor
Toronto, Ontario M5H 4E3, Canada
www.Harlequin.com

**Printed in U.S.A.**

The Spirit of the Lord God is upon me; because the Lord hath anointed me to preach good tidings unto the meek; he hath sent me to bind up the brokenhearted, to proclaim liberty to the captives, and the opening of the prison to them that are bound...

—*Isaiah* 61:1

This one's for Melissa, who saw the beauty within the concept and waited until it came to fruition. Thank you for your advice and ideas— they are a blessing to me and so many authors you've touched over the years! God bless you!

# Chapter One

*Hello, childhood.*

Jess Bristol sucked in a breath as she steered her rental car along mountain roads she hadn't seen in years. Curve upon curve, the lush Appalachian forest floated by on her right while a winter valley stretched wide on her left. Beautiful. Bucolic. Pastoral.

But when she hugged a bend that took her farther down the mountain, the Manhattan trauma doctor's breathing went tight for a different reason. The aftermath of the recent forest fire surrounded her. While some things had been completely consumed by the raging inferno, others had been randomly skipped over, leaving a tree here, bushes there. But not much had escaped the fire's wrath along this stretch, and the sleepy mountain town below—her hometown—had taken a nasty hit.

The late December fire had started high in the hills and swept down, fed by a strong east wind. Around her, the remnants of that two-day blaze lay haphazard and dark against the fresh falling snow.

Burned trees and ash peppered what had been a pristine landscape. She'd seen the news reports and her mother had sent several pictures of the recent disaster that had besieged the area. But the photos hadn't done it justice.

Devastation sprawled to her east, west and south. The fire's path had traveled straight for Kendrick Creek, the Tennessee mountain town she'd called home for over two decades. From here she could see the swath of wreckage along this edge of the fire. It hadn't burned the whole town, but it had ruined enough. In a little place like Kendrick Creek, it didn't take much to have a huge effect.

New York was different. And after spending twenty years in Manhattan, Jess was different. But she wasn't in New York now, so she paused and studied the sight below her.

It was bad. Her mother hadn't exaggerated, but then, she never had. Dr. Mary Bristol had taught her well when she'd taken the orphaned toddler under her wing forty years before. She'd stood by Jess through thick and thin.

Now it was Jess's turn.

She swallowed a sigh and lifted her chin. It wasn't about what she was giving up in Manhattan.

It was about what she was giving *back*. As she gazed down at the scarred town, her resolve faltered. Could she be a help to these folks? Or would her big city ways be more of a hindrance?

*That, girlie, is up to you now, isn't it?*

Granny Gee's voice came back to her. The words of wisdom the old mountain woman had passed on before she'd died. She hadn't had to die. Jess hadn't known that then. She understood it now. Granny was old-mountain stubborn and not about to travel any kind of distance for medical care. Good was good enough, she'd liked to say.

It wasn't, but there was no arguing with an up-mountain woman. Not then, and the same probably held true today.

So what good could Jess do here? Would the townspeople welcome her back while she helped her mother get Kendrick Creek Medical back up and running? Or would they scorn her "highfalutin" ways? She wasn't sure how it would go, but there, in the middle of the scorched and scarred town, one thing showed bright between the snowflakes despite the damage that had occurred. The church spire shone clean and white through the thinned expanse of downed trees and snow-crusted ash.

Her cell phone interrupted her thoughts. Her mother's number showed up in the display. "Hey, Mom."

"Are you really on your way home?" Mary asked. "Jess, darling, you don't have to do this. I'm fine. You know that. And we've got this. Everyone will come together to make things right again. They always do. It's how things are done here."

Mary Bristol had taken charge of an orphaned little girl when her family had been lost in a mountain road accident. She'd taken care of Jess from the first news of the wreck and seen her through the long hospitalization in Sevierville and weeks of physical therapy Jess had required as a result of the crushing blow she'd incurred that day. She hadn't been in a car seat. Probably not even in a seat belt.

Her adoptive mother had swooped in and taken charge like a she-bear, and Jess had gotten the best care, the best therapy, and had the best life. The thought of not helping her mother in a time of need was reprehensible. While Jess wasn't always the most tactful person, she wasn't a jerk, and she owed Mary Bristol absolutely everything. "Mom. You're stuck with me. And it's perfect timing because I'm between assignments right now. It's all good. I just caught sight of the town."

"A shock, isn't it? Even though Graham Tyler kept telling the town we were a sitting duck—but that's talk for another day. Drive safe, all right? If you're on the parkway, that road ices over real quick, honey."

Graham Tyler. He'd been two classes ahead of her at Kendrick Creek High School and a jerk. Maybe he'd changed. And maybe not. "I will. See you soon."

She turned off the Bluetooth and edged the SUV back onto the road.

Icy was right. Who'd have thought that pausing for five minutes to survey the damage would make a difference?

As she eased back onto the pavement, the tires slipped like water on glass. She gripped the wheel tight. Too tight, maybe. Then she hit the gas gently, like she'd been taught years before. Not gently enough, apparently.

The back tires slipped to the right.

Jess had been a great driver back in the day, but she

hadn't had to drive on snowy roads in over fifteen years. She turned the wheel.

*Wrong way.*

The vehicle didn't pull out of the skid, even with the SUV's computerized traction functions engaged. Her car spun at least once, maybe more, and careened into a slim, burned tree, back onto the road then back...

Sliding sideways...

Toward the open expanse of the timber-burned hillside that sloughed off in a long and possibly fatal drop. No guardrails blocked her slide. The forest that used to cradle the west side of the road was gone and Jess saw the tumbled and turned landslide as her possible demise.

She screamed.

She forgot everything she'd learned in driving school. For those quicksilver moments, all she saw was mortality and she was helpless to do anything about it.

Then the SUV spun one more time and, instead of the unblocked cliff before her, she found herself facing the scarred mountain slope above—from a vantage point that told her she was still in trouble.

"Mom?" She uttered the word carefully, in case the call was still connected. No voice answered her, so at least her mother had been spared the trauma of hearing her daughter's screams.

She glanced into the rearview mirror.

Snow filled the view. Snow that was falling well below her current line of vision.

That meant she was hovering close to the unprotected cliff side. Maybe too close to that sheer dropdown. Maybe not.

She unhooked her shoulder belt and turned slightly. That tiny action tipped the vehicle. Not good.

She hit the phone icon on the dashboard and sent out a 9-1-1 call. Should she sit and wait for the SUV to fall or risk climbing out?

Jess reached for the door handle but the SUV shifted again. From the view out her driver's-side window, she realized that while her tires were still on the ice-slick road's shoulder, the back end of her SUV was hanging over empty space.

Her heart jumped with an adrenaline rush.

She took a breath as the 9-1-1 call connected. When the operator asked, "What is your emergency?" Jess pretended she was in the ER and had to keep her cool to save a life. The pretense helped.

"This is Jess Bristol, I'm on the parkway, just above Kendrick Creek. My car spun out and I'm hovering on the edge of the cliff. The car moves every time I move and I'm afraid it's going over the edge if I try to get out."

"Are you visible from the road?"

"I am."

"And you can't exit the car?"

"Not safely."

"I've got help coming your way, miss, you're not too far out of town, but your mama has a police radio to stay up on things, and if she's hearing this call…well, you know her. She might be the first person there."

"Let's hope not, shall we?" The thought of her mother watching helplessly while Jess's SUV slipped over the cliff wasn't a welcome one. And the fact that her mother had probably heard the call-out and was heading her way reminded Jess that nothing was private in a small town. In her Long Island City condo, her life was her own. No one bothered her and she returned the favor.

Kendrick Creek was different.

A gust of wind barreled down from the hills above her. Her vehicle rocked. Did it shift?

Yes.

And not in a good way.

She closed her eyes and dropped her chin to pray. She hadn't prayed in a whole lot of years. More than she cared to admit. But this seemed like a real good time to start again.

*Dear God. Help me. Please. Just that. I don't know what to do and I need help. Please. Just send help.*

"Are you hurt?"

The strong male voice brought her chin up quickly.

Shane Stone.

There.

Outside her window.

The guy she'd ratted out in high school when a whole bunch of funds had disappeared from a local fundraiser. Shane Stone…a guy who'd filled a young girl's thoughts with all kinds of romantic notions until she'd seen him with that folded wad of bills like it was no big deal.

His eyes went wide as he surveyed her situation. Gorgeous eyes, still. Big blue eyes beneath shaggy brown hair that could use a trim but looked ruggedly appealing… And that heart-stopping face. Older. Wiser, maybe? And staring at her as if he'd just seen a blast from the past.

"Jess. Are you hurt?"

She shook her head and rolled down the window slightly. "No. But in a precarious situation, it seems."

"Story of my life," he muttered, but without the animosity she'd expected. He studied her then stepped back, gave the SUV a critical once-over, and reached out. "I'm going to open the door. When I do, the tires might slip. Your job is to have your seat belt off and be ready to jump, tumble or fly my way if the car moves. Got it?"

"But what if I make you fall and we both go over? Don't we have enough bad history already, Shane?"

He pointed to the side of the road. "I'm tethered." A wire cord went from his waist to the stump of a tree behind him. Above them, the lights of his pickup shone like beacons in the thickening snow. Another gust of wind raced down the mountain, twisting and turning the snow into less friendly conditions and she felt the force of the squall move the car, despite its being in Park with the emergency brake on. "I'd try to tow you, but there's no traction above or below, so I don't know what that would accomplish."

Jump.

*Into his arms.*

Talk about a leap of faith.

She didn't take time to think. Somehow she sensed that time wasn't on her side. She nodded briskly. "Let's do it."

He reached for the door. The handle clicked. He paused, rolled his eyes and met her gaze. "Unlock it."

Good grief. Where was her brain? She hit the switch and the lock clicked open. "Sorry, Shane."

* * *

Sorry?

*Now* she was sorry?

Those words were about a quarter century too late, but this wasn't the time to debate it because the next gust of wind might be enough to send the SUV over the edge. She couldn't see how close it was from her vantage point.

He could.

Flashing lights crept toward them from below, but he didn't dare wait for the volunteers. He understood thrust and weight and bearing and balance real well. They were huge components in good construction, and when Shane Stone built something, it was built to last.

But first he needed to save a life, it seemed. "Ready?"

Jess nodded.

"Go." He pulled the door open. He tried to swing it gently, but when he felt the SUV begin to slip away from him, gentle went out the window. He reached for her and barked, "Grab on!"

She tried to. She reached for his arm but the door got in the way and her hand jerked free and, for a few lightning-flash seconds, he saw her slipping away from him, just out of reach. "No! Grab, Jess!" As he yelled, he reached in and grabbed her as she grabbed him.

The SUV wrenched backward just as the wind gusted again. There was no turning back now.

He pulled hard. The rearward thrust of the car sucked at them as the door tried to close.

He held tight. When she finally came free, the momentum of her leap and the energy of his pull tumbled them both onto the ice-slicked road. Behind them, the SUV slipped over the edge and tumbled end-over-end onto a pile of burned debris lodged about halfway down the incline. Far enough to total the car. Far enough to easily end a life.

"Oh my gosh. Shane. Are you all right? Are you okay? I didn't mean to knock you over."

They were tangled together, cold but safe on the roadway as the receding echoes of the crashing car sounded around them.

He looked up into the beautiful caramel-brown eyes he'd been drawn to all those years ago. Before she pointed the finger of blame at him. Before he'd been forced to serve time for a crime he hadn't committed.

"You saved my life."

He wanted to say, *And you ruined mine*, but then he locked eyes with her.

Still beautiful. Still haunted. Still tinged with a sadness he'd never understood because she'd had everything a kid could ever want. And yet the fixer in him had wanted to fix things for her way back then. And the moment their eyes met and held, he realized he'd probably do the same now.

"All in a day's work," he told her. He waited while she righted herself before he pushed to his feet. Then he reached down and gave her a hand up before he unclasped the tether. "You okay?"

"Yes. Thanks to you. Shane, I—"

"Spare me, Jess. I'm not here to walk down memory

lane with you or anybody else. There're folks here that need help. A lot of help. I'm here to do a job and happened to run into you along the way."

Her eyes dimmed.

His fault.

But he understood his weakness for her. He'd have scoffed at that notion fifteen minutes ago, but he saw it now, plain as day.

She drew him. She'd done it back then. She did it now. But he wasn't an eighteen-year-old any longer, from a law-breaking family. He was Shane Stone, owner and now CEO of Stonefield Construction, a highly regarded business in Chevy Chase, Maryland. He'd purposely stayed far away from Kendrick Creek, and yet he was back again because there were people here who needed his help. Needed him. Just like he'd needed them, years ago.

"I was just going to thank you, Shane." Jess dusted the snow off her pants with ungloved hands.

She wasn't wearing a coat. She'd probably taken it off to drive, which now meant her coat and gloves were down the cliff.

He pulled off his Carhartt and held it out. "Here. You'll freeze."

"I'm good, thanks. And again, thanks for the rescue. My mother was spared finding her only child at the base of a ravine, so I owe you big-time."

She owed him nothing. And he wasn't about to take no for an answer. "Take the jacket, Jess. Please."

She faced him now and he realized two things.

First, she'd only gotten more beautiful in the twenty-five years that had passed, with the light brown hair that matched her eyes, and her pale complexion.

Second, she was just as stubborn as she had been back then and was never, ever, going to take the jacket. Maybe because it came from him.

Or maybe just to prove that she was in charge back then and she was still in charge now.

Except she wasn't.

He reached out, placed the thickly woven jacket over her shoulders and stood his ground. "I might be a jerk and an ex-con, but a good man doesn't stand by and let a lady freeze." He folded his arms but softened his gaze. Slightly. "I expect your mama is going to welcome you home."

He didn't wait for the rescue vehicles to make their last two hundred feet of the climb. He released the tether from the tree trunk, got into his truck, and eased down his side of the road, heading for town.

She was safe.

Help had arrived.

He had things to do.

As Shane passed the last of the emergency vehicles coming to her rescue, he knew that wasn't why he'd left.

He'd left because seeing Jess and saving her life showed him that the last thing he wanted to do was leave her. That had been enough of a reason to make a quick getaway. He had his life. She had hers. And if he had his way, they were never going to meet again.

Except that he was overseeing the rebuild on her mother's medical practice, and if Jess was here to help, that meant he'd be seeing her every single day. And that was way more than he'd bargained for when he headed south.

# Chapter Two

"Jess!" Mary Bristol hopped out of her SUV, nearly slipped on the ice, but kept her balance only by grabbing hold of the door handle. "Honey, are you all right? Your car! Jess, darling, you could have been killed!" she exclaimed as Jess shuffled across the slick surface toward her. Her mother grabbed hold of her as soon as she neared and pulled her in for a hug. "I can't even imagine the danger you were in, honey. Are you all right?"

"I am, thanks to Shane, and I'll be better when we get off this mountain." She hugged her mother as the bitter wind kicked up its heels again. The wind-and-snow combo was knife-cold and she slipped her arms into Shane's oversize jacket once her mother released her.

"Is that Shane's?"

Mary's question startled her. How would she know that? When Jess looked down, she saw the corporate logo: *Stonefield Construction*, the image of a home stitched above the words. She frowned and nodded. "He saved me." She didn't add that he might have been reluctant to save her considering their history because her mother already knew that.

"It says a lot that he's come back to help," Mary noted.

Jess didn't have time to answer because Grandy Martin was headed their way. A volunteer EMT who had been her mother's friend for years, Jess was surprised by how much the kind, caring man had aged. "You hurt, sweet thing?"

Sweet thing?

This sixtysomething medic hadn't just called a New York City ER doctor "sweet thing," had he?

She choked back a curt reply, which meant swallowing a fair amount of pride. "I'm okay, thank you, Mr. Martin. My car, however, leaves much to be desired."

"We'll leave that to the rental company to figure out," her mother said. "There's no sense risking folks' lives during a storm when the most precious thing in that car is standing right here. Grandy, can I take her home?"

"Go right ahead, Mary, we'll block the road and keep folks off it until the ice melts."

"Couldn't you just salt it?" Jess asked. With temps in the mid-twenties a generous coating of rock salt would melt the danger away.

"It's mighty early in the season to get too deep into our allotment," he told her. "Use it too early and we get an ice storm in March…well, then we're in a fix. And not too many take this way in winter. Most come down low."

"I'll be sure to remember that," Jess replied.

When Mary put light pressure on her arm, Jess stopped talking. She knew she sounded snippy, and she didn't want to be. She'd started to round her mother's SUV when Mary reached out and gave Grandy a hug.

"Thank you and the guys for coming up here, Grandy. I don't know what this town would do without our volunteers. I know you must all be tired after the fight we've had on our hands this past week."

The fire.

Jess hung her head, literally. She'd been up in arms about road conditions when these people had fought tooth-and-nail to save what they could of their town, their livelihoods, and their homes. Shame cut deep. "Grandy, I am most grateful for your efforts," she said sincerely. "And you won't worry about that car, will you? I don't want anyone getting hurt."

"You got personal stuff in there, Jess?"

"My medical bag, my suitcase and a duffel. Nothing I can't wait on."

Grandy shifted in the thickening snow, a worried look on his face. "This is supposed to turn to rain tomorrow down-mountain, but it's slated for snow, snow, and more snow up here."

"Then we'll dig it out when it stops." Jess hated saying that. She never went anywhere unprepared. It was against her nature. Today she had little choice.

"You go get warm. And you're welcome, Jess."

He gave her a caring look, like a dad gives his beloved kids on TV, total fiction in Jess's estimation. In all her life, she'd never had the love or presence of a father. For whatever reason, it hadn't been in the cards.

But she'd had her mother, and a more staunch supporter had never been born.

Jess climbed into the passenger side of her mother's SUV and held her hands directly in front of the heater. "I expect we have to go up to go down, correct?" she said as Mary took her place behind the wheel. The winding two-lane road and missing guardrails allowed no room for a K-turn under such icy conditions.

"That's exactly what we'll do," her mother replied. She put the vehicle in gear and proceeded forward carefully. When they got to a right-hand parking area, she made the turnaround then eased the SUV down the road at a necessarily slow rate that made Jess restless because going slow hadn't been in her repertoire for a long time.

"I'm surprised you didn't take Route 321 when you got to Wilton Springs," Mary said as the car curved right then left then right again, snaking its way to the road below.

"This seemed shorter."

"Ah."

Jess sighed and laid her head back against the headrest. "Dumb, in retrospect."

"Well, you've been gone a long time. And they just got this cleared. It was closed for a couple of days with fire debris. They had to prioritize the town and the emergency services surrounding it."

"Of course. I think it says a lot that they got the parkway cleared as quickly as they did. Although my GPS was not happy."

"A storm messes things up," Mary told her, not taking her eyes off the deepening snow on the road. "They put warnings out for visitors because the next thing you know, your GPS leads you down a gravel road to nowhere."

"As odd as this sounds, it does the same thing in parts of New York," Jess acknowledged. "The buildings in Lower Manhattan are so high that you lose the satellite signal, and all of a sudden you're in a maze of tiny streets and have no idea which way to go."

"I can't imagine." Mary breathed out softly. "It amazes me every time I come up there, and while it's always a thrill to visit, I can't wait to get back home to my mountains. These hills draw me, Jess. But not you. You've always liked the challenge of big schools, big cities, big hospitals. Are you eventually going to tell me why you were free to come down here?" Once she navigated the turn to Kendrick Creek, Mary glanced at Jess. "What's going on?"

"I left my job."

Silence stretched the limits of the car. "What happened, Jess?"

"I got downsized."

Her mother winced, but it wasn't a sad wince. It was mama bear anger that drew her brows together. "Because of the cancer?"

Jess didn't want to talk about it, but life had taken that option away from her. "They replaced me on research projects, on grant proposals, and then the promotion I'd worked toward for nearly ten years went to a younger woman who didn't have to take nearly a year off for breast cancer treatment."

"Oh, Jess. How did they justify that? How does a

hospital with a nationally recognized cancer center turn its back on one of its own?"

"Well, it's New York. And if you can't get the job done in their time frame, there are a dozen smart and motivated doctors from all over the world waiting to take your place."

A black pickup passed them just then. Shane's black truck? But then another one followed, and another, so she had no idea which, if any, was Shane's. And why were there so many of the same trucks here in town? "I'm on a leave of absence and, putting out applications to other major medical centers. Cleveland. Baltimore. Boston."

"The South needs great doctors, too, you know."

"I know, Mom. It's just—"

"It's all right, Jess." Her mother reached over and patted her hand. "It's always been all right. You go where the good Lord leads you."

Jess peered out at the thickening snow as they drove through the sorry-looking small town.

Her mother was a steadfast believer, but in all her time in New York, Jess hadn't missed the church services she'd been raised on. She'd spent years walking by fairly empty churches and cathedrals in a city of millions. Church? Who had time for church when life in the city moved at breakneck speed?

As her mother turned down Duck Hollow Road, the lights from that little country church shone like a golden beacon in the snowy night. Yellow light splayed across unbroken snow like one of those old Christmas cards.

In that instant, Jess felt like she was in one of those nostalgic cards.

And it felt good.

Shane didn't need anyone to tell him that climbing down a fire-scarred mountainside to retrieve Jess's personal possessions was downright stupid and dangerous, not to mention ridiculously cold as the sun's light faded.

They'd closed the road and his Maryland nanny had his niece, Jolie, and nephew, Sam, safe and sound in a clean little motel north of town, away from the fire's destruction. That gave him some time and leverage. His partner had helped rig a winch. Pete Field and several others had come south with him when they'd heard about the destructive fire. Good men who could have been biding their time on unemployment in Maryland, but who'd wanted to help. The kind of people he'd surrounded himself with once he'd served his time.

He rappelled down the hill, attached the tether, and Pete hauled the bags up the incline one by one, until all of Jess's things were loaded into the back seat of his work truck.

"You're covered in snow, man." Surprise widened Pete's eyes when Shane finally made it back up the hill nearly an hour after he'd begun the climb down. "You've got to be frozen."

"Stealing Hubbel's coat helped," said Shane. He wasn't about to admit how cold he was because Pete already thought his mission was crazy. "Thanks for operating the pulley for me, Pete. I owe you."

"You brought me on when I got out of prison," Pete

replied. He'd gone to jail as a reckless teen, mad at the world and always ready to fight. "And brought me back to the faith my mama tried to teach me. You don't owe me a thing, Shane. Not now. Not ever."

Shane bumped knuckles with the guy who'd shared his cell over twenty years ago. "Moving forward, my man."

"Always."

It had become their mantra in prison. It had eased the long days that melded into weeks, then months, then years, but the pair had used every opportunity to better themselves. And here they were, running an award-winning construction firm that focused on the American dream: a home.

The irony that two men who'd never had what could be called a real home were building that very thing for others wasn't lost on Shane. "I'll drop you off, then take these things over to Doc Bristol's."

"Drop them first, it's on the way," Pete argued. "Otherwise you're out driving in the snow an extra hour when you don't have to be."

Pete made a good point. The work crew he'd brought south was housed in the same motel back near Wilton Springs. No one in Kendrick Creek had their mountain cabins open for rental right now. The little motel had worked for the past two days. It wasn't a long-term solution, but it served the purpose until he could set up a different arrangement. "All right. Thanks, Pete."

He pulled into Mary's driveway a few minutes later, rounded the curve and paused the truck by her rustic wooden porch. "I'll just be a minute."

"I'll be here."

He grabbed the duffel from the back seat and hooked it over his shoulder, maneuvered a carry-on-size suitcase, a coat that smelled of wild honey, and the small black bag. Then he hip-checked the door shut.

"I'd be glad to help," Pete called to him.

"Got it, but thanks." This wasn't a social call. This was simply something that needed to be done once he'd heard in town that it would be days before anyone could get down the mountain to retrieve Jess's stuff.

He climbed the steps and crossed the wood-planked porch that fit the setting and Doc Bristol. Strong and rugged with a touch of whimsy. He had to set a bag down to hit the doorbell. He was bending to retrieve it when the thick wooden door swung open.

Shane raised his gaze and his heart stood still when he saw Jess.

She'd ditched his jacket.

She was wearing pajama pants and a long-sleeved T-shirt. The sleeves hit mid arm, which meant they were probably Mary's pajamas. Jess was a good five inches taller than her mother.

But it wasn't the casual pj's, backlit by a flickering fire that held him riveted.

It was her lack of hair.

When he realized what it meant, he felt like he'd been sucker-punched. Stupid, stinking cancer stalking yet another beautiful person. He straightened and handed her the small bag.

"You went back for my stuff?" she whispered, raising her eyes to his. Realization changed her demeanor.

She brought a hand to her head and grimaced. "My current hairstyle is courtesy of breast cancer. I'm still guessing whether my hair comes back curly or straight. Gray or brown. And yes, what you saw earlier was a wig that needed drying after being in the snow."

A wig.

His heart hurt for her. Not because she'd lost her hair, but because he'd lost his sister to cancer eighteen months earlier and he understood what Jess was going through. "You've had surgery?"

She nodded.

"Radiation?"

"Six weeks. I was stage two before it was discovered."

That meant it wasn't contained. "And then the chemo?"

"You know too much about this," she said as she swung the door wider and reached for the second bag. "We're letting all the heat out, Shane."

"Chrissie died a year and a half back. Thyroid cancer."

"Oh, Shane, I'm sorry."

His turn to grimace. "She was alone with two kids when she got diagnosed. Her husband had left the year before, so I brought her to Baltimore. She got treatment and the kids had family close by. She got six good years with me and the kids, so I try to be grateful for that, but it wasn't enough. You know?"

"Yeah. I know."

Of course she knew. She was living it. "I'm sorry about this, Jess."

She squared her shoulders. "It happens."

"Sometimes there's no explaining or understanding God's timing." She made a face. "You don't embrace that idea?" he asked.

"Let's just say that if a patient thinks prayer will help, I encourage it. A good doctor understands we don't just treat the symptoms. We treat the mental, physical, emotional and spiritual, even if we're not believers."

"Well, this believer is putting you on his prayer list." He set down the third bag as Mary came into the room. She lifted her brows in surprise.

"I heard voices." She smiled at him then noticed the bags. "Oh, Shane, did you go after Jess's stuff?"

"No big deal." He raised his hands, palms out, and backed toward the door.

"Stay for supper," Mary urged.

"Pete's in the truck. He helped me. Gotta get back to the kids, but thank you."

"Then at least let me pack food for all of you." Sympathy marked Mary's expression. "I have beef stew and fresh bread. Will they eat that?"

The rich scent of cooked beef made him want to stay, but he shouldn't. Not with so much to do. "Nettie fed them already. But thank you. I sincerely appreciate the offer." Annette "Nettie" Bondi, the kids' nanny, would be heading back north soon. She had a grandbaby due next week, though she'd made the trip to Tennessee to help get them settled. Lack of power had delayed that, but full service had been restored to the valley that afternoon. Now he just had to find a place for him and his workers to stay.

"Then you and Pete should have supper here."

"I'm sure he's got things to do, Mom," Jess chimed in.

He did. He needed to figure out specs on the three buildings he'd toured today, including Kendrick Creek Medical, Mary's clinic, and draw up supply lists. Yet something about the way Jess tried to push him off made him square his shoulders. "Actually, it's nothing that can't wait an hour or two and I'm sure Pete would love a home-cooked meal. Me, too."

Mary smiled, delighted. "Perfect! I'll set two more places."

He regretted his rash decision the minute he'd said the words, but he couldn't back out now.

Jess skewered him with a look.

He ignored it.

He'd watched Chrissie trudge a rough path twice. Once with her original diagnosis and then, when the cancer resurged five years later, in her long, hard fight before she went home to God. She'd left Shane a niece and nephew to raise, ages eight and ten now, two kids that had called him "Pops" from the time they were little. It had been a joke back then. The joke became reality when their mom died.

He knew about fighting the disease firsthand. And while he and Jess had no love lost for one another, he was pretty sure her mother would welcome some support because watching someone you love suffer was way harder than suffering yourself. He strode out to the pickup and shut the engine off. "We've been invited for supper."

"Don't have to ask me twice." Pete bounded out

of the truck. "Anything that isn't slapped across a stainless-steel counter is a huge step up." He followed Shane and entered Mary's eclectic home.

When he spotted Jess, Pete didn't miss a beat. "Ma'am, I'm so grateful at the thought of real food that if you wanted me to go down that hill and haul that car up on my shoulders, I'd do it."

Jess laughed.

Shane's pulse spiked the minute he heard that sound.

He'd fallen for that laugh a long time ago, and to hear it now, understanding her condition, made it even more special. "No need for that level of heroics," she assured him, and stretched out her hand. "I'm Jess Bristol. I've come home to help my mother get the clinic back in order."

Unlike Shane's look of surprise, her condition didn't make Pete miss a beat. "It'll be a team effort to set things right, and my partner here has set a twelve-week calendar to get stuff done so we don't mess with our contracts back home. Folks keep telling me this is a get-it-done kind of town, so I think we'll be okay."

"Wonderful." She reached over and nonchalantly slipped a pale blue knit hat over her head as if covering baldness was no big deal.

It wasn't, but Shane couldn't help remembering the feel of her long, curly brown hair. How if you stretched out one of those curls, the straightened lock came halfway down her back, but sprang back up to rest on her shoulders when you let go.

He'd dreamed of that as a teen. She'd have thought him silly then, because a kid related to infamous crime families in nearby Newport, the same group that tried to get Chrissie in their law-breaking clutches, shouldn't have a crush on the town doctor's daughter. Especially not when she was not only voted most likely to succeed, she'd gone and done it.

But when she looked up at Pete and laughed at something he said, something akin to jealousy ran through him.

Seeing Jess brought up a whole bunch of what-ifs. Like, what if her deposition hadn't put him in jail? Could there have been something between them?

No.

His head understood that. It always had. So why couldn't his heart get with the program?

Shane had no idea.

# *Chapter Three*

As a kid, Jess'd had a print of *Peaceable Kingdom* on her bedroom wall, the artistic rendering of carnivores and herbivores getting along. It was based on some Bible verse about the lion laying down with the lamb.

*As if.*

In reality, the lion would make an easy dinner of the lamb, but sitting at a supper table with the man she'd put in jail reminded her of that picture.

*You did nothing wrong. You testified about what you saw. Kids make mistakes. They pay for them. End of story.*

She'd tried to convince herself of that. It worked most of the time, but every now and again, her brain took her back to that night, seeing Shane with that huge wad of money then imagining him sitting in jail. The knowledge that her words had sent a man, barely more than a boy, to prison, made her gut ache.

"So, Pete, have you and Shane been working together long?" Mary asked as she served up bowls of rich beef stew.

"Shane got out two years before I did," Pete began.

If Jess reacted to his words, he was gentleman enough not to notice. "He got a job with a contractor near Baltimore who needed good help and was willing to give us a shot. Then when Shane noticed some zombie properties here and there, we decided to branch out on our own." He spotted her confused expression and added, "Abandoned places. Waiting for some TLC. We'd fix them up and flip them before it became a thing."

"So you worked together to build a business," Jess observed.

"We employ several ex-cons," Shane said simply. "Guys who needed a hand up, not a handout."

"Shane." Mary reached a hand to his arm as Jess passed the basket of freshly baked rolls. Mary's warm expression of approval hit Jess's midsection. "That's wonderful. What a marvelous way of completing the circle of caring."

Mary turned to Pete. She didn't see Shane's reaction to her words. But Jess did. She was about to say something, but Pete jumped in.

"Ma'am, this is beyond a delight," he exclaimed. "I'm never a fussy eater, but that doesn't make me less appreciative about the wonder of this meal."

"I expect it was cold up on that mountain," she said.

Pete laughed. "Well, I was operating the winch and had the truck cab to warm my hands and my face, but Shane was the one who went down the hill in the ice and cold on the end of a tether."

"You needed a tether to get down there?" Jess pictured the wrecked SUV midway down the steep incline and frowned. "Of course you did. Shane, what were you thinking? What if you'd been hurt?"

"I wasn't," he told her in a mild tone, and it was just mild enough to ruffle her feathers. "And you needed your things. You're a doctor. You're here to help. And Mary's clothes don't exactly fit, in case you haven't noticed."

She saw the glint of amusement in his eyes when he looked her way.

"A little short in the sleeve is all. Well…" Jess glanced down. "The legs, too. But you could have waited until tomorrow."

"One thing life's taught me is never wait until tomorrow and don't leave folks hanging. The lessons I learned growing up on the mountain have never left me. And never will," he vowed as he buttered a third roll. "Be fair, work hard, jump in as needed."

"Even though some folks treated your family poorly." Mary made the quiet observation as she waited for a spoonful of stew to cool.

"My extended family gave people reason to talk, sure. It wasn't who I was, or who I am, but it's old news now. Jesus did mention that seventy times seven rule, right?"

"My kind of hero." Mary raised her spoon in salute.

"No hero. Just a guy who wants to help get people back on their feet down here." Shane stood. "We've got to push on. Mary, can I help with dishes?"

"No, sir, you cannot," she told him firmly. "You men get on. I'll see you tomorrow."

"Tomorrow?" Jess asked.

Mary raised both brows, surprised. "Of course."

Jess didn't need Mary's puzzled expression to figure out the obvious. Shane would be overseeing the reconstruction of her mother's clinic, which meant he'd be underfoot every day. Jess tried wrapping her brain around that and couldn't because she hadn't bargained for this.

"I'm going to get the church back in order," noted Pete. "With a stretch of good weather, we can get a lot done before we need to head back home. Once the outside's secure, the weather don't matter much except to our shoes, so I'm hoping the church can be done soon."

"Gentlemen, thank you again for gathering Jess's things," her mother said. "And for staying for supper."

"Pure pleasure, ma'am." Pete bowed slightly in a sweet gesture of respect. "Good night to you both."

"I'll see you tomorrow, Mary." Shane spotted his jacket hanging by the woodstove. He picked it up, felt the warmth and smiled. "All dry. Thank you," he said to Jess.

Was it his words that spurred the flicker of her heart? His gaze? She wasn't sure.

"I'll get the generators hooked up to give us power," he told her mother. "It should be light enough to get things rolling by eight or so."

"This early in January, more like eight thirty, but whatever works for you, Shane. And I'll be right across the street if you need anything. Some of my friends helped me set up a makeshift clinic in the empty law office."

"Whatever works in a pinch, right?"

He strode through the small house. When he got

to the front door, he turned and seemed surprised to find Jess behind him. Surprised and almost happy, she thought. But then the happiness faded. "I wanted to thank you again," she told him.

He brushed it off. "None needed. Just doing a good turn."

"Shane—"

"Gotta go. Thanks for supper. And..." He reached out and touched the three bright-toned flowers crocheted onto the side of her chemo cap. "Nice hat."

Was it the way he said it? Or the fact that he treated her and the hat as if a new normal was still just normal?

None of this was normal. The fire, the job, the stupid cancer.

None of that mattered when Shane talked to her. The sweet gesture made her heart skip as if lighter. "Thanks."

He met her gaze again, briefly. Just long enough for her to see the compassion in his eyes.

She didn't want him feeling sorry for her. She didn't want anyone feeling sorry for her. She'd faced her almost year-long treatment pretty much alone at one of the best facilities in the nation. She had so much to be grateful for. Pity annoyed her, but it wasn't pity she saw in Shane's eyes.

It was understanding. As if he knew her, better than others did. As if he got it.

But how could that be when every time she looked at him, regret flooded her brain like the streets of Lower Manhattan in Superstorm Sandy.

\* \* \*

*I hate cancer.*

The thought hit Shane as he started the truck.

He'd read the guilt in her face when their eyes met. Guilt over something that had happened a long time ago, an emotion she shouldn't feel. He knew that. She didn't. He'd purposely left the past in the past. Faith and friendship had bolstered him.

But now he was back where every corner held a memory, every sight took him to a childhood that left so much to be desired.

He pulled into the motel parking lot, said good-night to Pete and knocked on Nettie's door. She opened it with a wide smile. "Shane, how did everything go today? Were you able to get a good look at the damaged areas?"

She didn't ask about housing for the kids as he stepped inside and closed the door, but Jolie wasn't about to let him off so easily. She wasn't happy. She hadn't been happy for a while, and he wasn't sure how to fix that. How did one fix the loss of a mother for a ten-year-old and an eight-year-old?

He couldn't, but he'd promised Chrissie he'd do his best.

She'd hugged him because she knew he meant it, but his lack of success with Jolie weighed heavy on his shoulders.

She stood on the opposite side of the motel room and folded her arms with a look of expectation. "Are we staying here forever, Pops?"

He shook his head. "Another day or two is all, until I find a place to rent, sugar."

"I mean this place. This town. This state." Disdain oozed out of her pores. "This isn't our home. It's not even close to our home, it's so far away. I don't know why we couldn't stay with the Platts. They invited us because they like us."

The Platts were a lovely family in their Maryland neighborhood that had offered their help when Shane decided to come to Tennessee. "Because I need you with me," Shane told her mildly.

Sammy skipped out of the bathroom just then, freshly showered and in superhero pajamas. The eight-year-old vaulted over a small suitcase and landed at Shane's feet with an expression of absolute love. "Pops! Nettie took us shopping and got us some summer stuff because she said it gets hot pretty quick down here and we might need shorts and stuff before we go home, and I said that would be great even though it's not warm now." He made an "eek!" face at the snowy window. "Do you think she's kidding?"

Sammy's love and trust had been a given from the beginning, way back when Chrissie's first treatments had begun. Jolie was different. She held back, and if Shane had an easy way to help her see the good in life, he'd use it, but it didn't exist. Lately he'd been wondering what he was doing wrong with her, but how could he figure that out?

*Faith.*

He hugged Sammy close. "You smell good, she's not kidding, and even though it's snowing now, that's all right. Spring comes early in Tennessee and those shorts will come in handy, I promise you. And the way you're growing, buddy, you're going to need new things."

Beyond the window the motel's somewhat garish Christmas lights mocked thoughts of spring. Sporadic holiday lighting brightened the road between Kendrick Creek and Wilton Springs, a reminder that Christmas felt like a long time ago. Not five simple days.

Sam hugged him.

Jolie didn't. She looked like she wanted to, but then she turned, picked up a book, and curled up on the far bed. "I'll try to find us a place tomorrow," he promised her. He crossed the room, bent and kissed her forehead. She didn't look up. Punishing him for uprooting them, no doubt. "Love you, JoJo."

The old nickname usually made her smile.

Not tonight.

Nettie sent him an understanding look as Sam hugged him then scrambled onto the rollaway bed. "This bed is so cool!" He laughed from his spot low on the floor. "I can fall off a thousand times and never get hurt once!"

"Good to hear." He kissed Sammy and gave Nettie a wave before he left the room. "I'm right next door if you need me," he reminded her.

Later on, when he stepped outside for a breath of cold, crisp mountain air after he'd crunched way too many numbers, the windows of their room were dark.

Had he been wrong to bring them here?

Maybe.

But he'd done it for their own good. And his. He only hoped it had been the right thing to do.

## Chapter Four

The floor was ice cold when Jess pulled open the first-floor bedroom door at seven o'clock the next morning and Shane Stone was already sitting at her mother's old maple table.

He looked up. Met her stare. She stood still, her eyes locked on his as her mother turned from the coffeepot. She set a mug in front of Shane then motioned Jess over. "Shane has been drafting plans for the clinic. Come see what you think."

She pulled the cap into place, and when Shane's sympathetic eyes followed the action, she squared her shoulders because cancer didn't define her. It was simply something that had happened to her.

Her mother sat on one side of Shane. Jess had no choice but to take the chair on his left. The minute she did, she realized no man should smell that good at 7:10 a.m.

But he did. Some kind of spicy goodness mixed with outdoor air. The kind of air she'd forgotten after years of being cloistered in a city of millions, but a scent she remembered now with Shane at her side. It was all she could do not to breathe him in, inhale the essence, but the situation was already weird enough. "You've had time to do all this?" she asked, eyeing the pencil-scratched sketches, not trying to hide the skepticism in her voice.

His notes weren't the architectural renderings she'd expected. It was little more than quick-dashed lines and tiny numerical measurements at various points. But on another piece of paper, the dollar and cents of the situation were typed out in firm, neat rows with a tally that ate up every bit of her mother's insurance money and a chunk more besides.

While Mary made a comfortable living in the valley, Jess suspected her philanthropic nature hadn't allowed much left over for retirement, much less emergencies. "Can you really assume those figures?" She motioned to the cost sheet. "From that?" She pointed to the rough rendering in front of him.

"Do you need a schematic to remove a bullet?" he replied. The gentle chiding sent a stab of regret through her. "Your mother is expanding the office to include two more exam rooms and a bathroom, with an additional two hundred square feet of clerical space. We're simply reflecting the north half of the office to the south half in a mirror image setup and repairing the fire damage to the original structure. With appropriate upgrades, of course."

"You need more space, Mom?" Jess might have

sounded too surprised because her mother shifted both brows up instantly.

"I may be nearing seventy, my dear, but I'm not exactly in my dotage."

"I didn't mean—"

Mary didn't let her finish. "And *because* I'm nearing retirement age, I want the practice to look good to potential buyers, so I'm investing now to reap rewards later."

"Risk versus reward," Shane offered by way of explanation. "ROI," he added, deliberately focusing on Jess. "That's return on—"

"I know what return on investment is," she replied, practically rolling her eyes at him.

"Good."

Jess couldn't quite let it go. "Is there enough business in the area to expand like that, though? Will the numbers add up to a potential buyer when you're ready, Mom?"

Mary passed the small stoneware pitcher of cream as she replied. "You haven't been back for a long time, Jess. You'll be surprised to see how the town has grown. We've become a community of haves and have-nots in the past dozen years."

She didn't screen her doubt quickly enough because her mother offered her the kind of look that always squelched, even though Jess was forty-three years old.

"Spillover from the huge rise of business from Sevierville down to Gatlinburg, and, of course, there's Dollywood," Mary added. "Those places have gotten crowded, so folks are building north and south of the towns. It's only thirty minutes to the parkway from here, and we've got plenty of space. Over five hundred thousand people have moved to Tennessee in the last nine years, and the valley is feeling the growth."

"And don't forget the Yankees coming south to retire," Shane interjected, then directed his attention to Mary. "With the right kind of shops, folks would take the turn down here, grab food and gas up and shop before they get on their way again. It's an opportunity waiting to happen. Some smart person is going to see that and capitalize on it," he finished as he reached for his coffee mug.

"Having someone with the right mindset and skill set to do that would be an answer to prayer." Mary spoke softly, but she aimed that wise look straight at Shane and you didn't have to be a rocket scientist to read her train of thought. "Something to think on, isn't it? And pray on, most likely. So…" She perched her reading glasses on her nose and tapped the paper closest to her. "Let's talk numbers."

Shane was skilled at talking numbers, but it was difficult with Jess Bristol sitting nearby.

She leaned her head forward to see the figures, and the scent of her didn't waft over him. It enveloped him, like a misty mountain morning.

He couldn't lean away because Mary flanked his right, and he had a job to do, but the fragrant air called to him. He kept his face toward Mary and pretended Jess's sweet essence wasn't driving him crazy.

"I'm going to suggest heated floors, Mary." He

pointed to a notation on the second page. "Patients really appreciate warm floors during the colder months and a percentage of high reviews for similar practices in the eastern Tennessee region mentioned that. Since we've got to do a major overhaul, I'm suggesting adding that in. The insurance settlement is generous enough to cover the initial costs because we're repurposing as much material as we can to use on other projects."

"That's amazing, Shane," Jess offered. "I hate to think of how much we throw away these days. There's got to be a way to do it better, right?"

He glanced left, into Jess's eyes. Big mistake.

Tiny spikes of gold sparked the tawny tones that used to match her hair. The hair was gone, but the eyes—

He remembered them well. Too well. With longing when he was just graduating from high school, then with such utter disappointment whenever she'd see him later, while he was being investigated for grand theft. A theft he'd paid the price for, and something he'd do again if he had to, because his sacrifice had given Chrissie the opportunity to turn her life around.

"Throwing things away never set well with me." It took effort to keep his reply generic, but he did it. "Use it up, wear it out."

"Agreed." Mary noted the final tally with her finger. "Will that cover everything, or do we need a padding percentage? I've got a small retirement account and I can—"

"Mom, you are not using your retirement account for this." Mary and Jess faced off over the table.

"I've got money. I've built a portfolio. I'll pay the

difference and you keep your money invested," Jess pressed.

"Jess, that's not going to happen." Mary's tone was mild but Shane recognized the steel behind the velvet. "I'm comfortable enough."

"You could simply invest in the practice," Shane suggested to Jess. He pushed his chair back slightly to see both women. "That could work."

"I'm not staying." Jess, turned his way, didn't see the flash of hurt in Mary's eyes. Shane did.

"You don't need to be physically present to be an investor, right?" He kept his tone cool.

She flushed. "Sorry. I misread your words. You mean investing in Kendrick Creek Medical as a business prospect."

"Exactly." Shane didn't add chill to his voice but he didn't warm it up, either. While Jess might not love her hometown, Mary was an integral part of the community. "When Mary sells the business at a profit, you get your money back and she doesn't have to disturb her 401K until she's ready to retire."

"I don't need Jess to do this," Mary remarked. "I'm not afraid of investing in the town I love, especially when we've hit hard times."

"But there is good sense in Shane's idea," Jess told her. "I've got the money, I'd actually like to diversify some of my investments and now is the perfect time. Why not this?" She posed the question to her mother. "My money couldn't possibly be safer anywhere than it is with you."

Mary started to object, then didn't. She looked at Jess. And then she looked at Shane.

Then she simply nodded, as if quietly trusting everything to work out.

How Shane wished he could do that right now.

He pressed his hands against the table and stood. "Let's finish this on site, all right?"

"Sounds good." Mary stood, too. "We'll meet you there in fifteen minutes. Then we can head across the street to my temporary offices."

"Pete just texted that the generators are up and running and we have emergency lighting. So, yes, I'll see you up the road." He headed out quickly.

When Jess and Mary arrived a few minutes later, he swung the door open. Before they came through, he handed Mary a hard hat, then turned to Jess. He hesitated just long enough for her to respond.

"The hat's not going to hurt my head, Shane, if that's what you're wondering." She reached for the hard hat to make her point. "I've got my chemo cap firmly in place. But thank you for the kindness," she added. "It's really nice of you."

"I hate cancer." He kept his tone flat.

She took the hat and settled it in place. "I'm not a big fan of it, myself." She grinned.

Mary interjected, "You said your nanny is heading back north soon, Shane. What are you going to do about the kids?"

"I called Devlyn McCabe, like you suggested." Devlyn had been a classmate of Jess's back in the day. "She said she'd love to help out. Said it would help to keep her busy," he added. "Now we just need to find a place to stay."

"Renting can get costly," Mary observed as he taped copies of his sketches to the inside wall of the less damaged area.

"Costs work out," Shane told her. "They always do. My oldest is less than thrilled with my arrangements. She would have preferred to stay with friends in Maryland. My negative response downgraded my standing, I'm afraid."

"Kids." Mary winked at Jess. "They're so sure they know what's best."

"Truth," Shane quipped as he applied one last piece of tape. "Let's just say I respect their opinions, but seeing sacrificial love in action is a better lesson than hearing about it from the pulpit."

Jess met his gaze. Behind her, industrial fans blew air out broad windows as the men prepped one area for renovation and the other side for demolition. "Hard work builds character."

"Always has," Shane replied. He moved forward with Mary, pointing out his thoughts on the reconstruction.

The building reeked. Would the smell bother Jess? He hoped not.

He watched Jess make notes in her phone as she snapped pics of the burned-out rooms, the water damage, the melted vinyl and ruined cabinetry. Would she only see the destruction here? Or would she see her mother's devotion through all the rubble? He hoped so.

Her mother had put her blood, sweat and tears into this place. When he was a boy, the practice had been in the front of an old hardware store just up the road a piece. The store was still there, damaged but not gone. He turned to point out an idea when the outer door banged open.

"Help!"

The Trembeths stood framed in the doorway, a whole lot older than they'd been when he'd gone to prison. Ed was struggling to keep Hassie upright. Ed looked past Jess and yelled to her mother, "Mary, I need help and I need it fast!"

"Ed. Hassie." Mary moved toward the door.

Jess was quicker. She charged forward. The acrid smell was pushed aside by the blast of cold, fresh air, but Hassie listed left, took one breath and started to faint.

Jess got to her just in time.

She supported her with one arm. Shane took the other.

Together they got Hassie outside in the fresh air and into the back of Mary's SUV.

It felt right to work with Jess.

It shouldn't. They had a past that couldn't be reconciled, he had secrets he needed to keep, and Jolie and Sam had dealt with cancer once.

That made it a no-brainer.

And yet, having her here, working nearby, would be a constant reminder of what couldn't possibly happen.

He'd dealt with that twenty-five years before when he turned and saw that look of disappointment in her eyes when she caught him with that money.

He had no intention of dealing with it again.

# Chapter Five

E.R. instinct kicked in. "Mom, grab my bag from the front seat," Jess ordered. She yanked the hard hat off and handed it to Shane. "Do we have oxygen that wasn't ruined?"

"Across the street."

"I'm on it." Shane settled the woman into the back of the now open SUV, then ran across the road.

The snow had stopped overnight, and the new day shone with bright sun, but the reflection off the fresh snow was blinding after being in the soot-darkened offices.

Mary thrust an oxygen meter into Jess's hand then the stethoscope.

"Low oxygen," Jess reported. "Pulse is erratic. Was she in the fire?" she asked Ed Trembeth.

He nodded. "I was workin' and by the time I got out to Kendall Mills Road they had it blocked and they wouldn't let me through the main way," he told her. "By the time I took back fields, Hassie had gotten the kids out of the house and down the road, but she got lost back inside trying to get the littlest one. She'd curled up in a corner. She was all right, but they said Hassie might have gotten a lot of smoke."

"Was she taken in?" asked Jess.

The man looked blank.

Mary rephrased the question for him. "Did they take her to the hospital, Ed?"

"Wouldn't go," he told them. Regret laced his voice. "She said whatever was wrong with her would ease itself, and she had two kids to take care of. Three, counting me, is what she told them, and they kinda laughed, but you think she shoulda gone, Mary?"

Jess was about to bark an affirmative answer, and maybe say something she shouldn't, when her mother intervened. "It's expensive, Ed. I know where you're coming from, and I know that Hassie's as strong as they come, but she should have let them treat her. Now that it's been a few days, we could have an infection that could cause problems with her heart. It could do a lot of stuff. Let us work on her. Bring her across the way, out of the cold."

"To the law offices of Aiden G. Cromwell?" Jess asked as Shane brought the battery-operated oxygenator alongside. "Mom, shouldn't we—"

"I unlocked the door." Shane handed Mary the key. "What's best for her?" he asked, turning to Jess. "Me carrying her or me backing the SUV as close to the door as you can get?"

"You back it up, I'll ride with, but there better be a real good reason why we're not sending this woman to the nearest hospital in the back of an ambulance, Mom," Jess stormed. She took a spot alongside the old woman.

Cold air bathed them and a quick breeze made it worse as Shane backed the SUV over the paved road and up to the curb. The law office was on a sharp diagonal from Mary's office, and despite three nearby buildings almost completely torched, and four others badly damaged, this two-office building was largely unscathed.

When Jess followed Shane inside, warmth and cleanliness surrounded her. She moved forward, following her mother into the back office. One office was being used as an exam room. The other as a tiny clinic.

Two beds stood side by side, separated by a homemade curtain suspended from a plastic rod above. Shane gently laid the woman on the first bed, and Jess did a quick recheck on vitals while Mary set the oxygenator on the small side table. She set the nasal tube in place and turned the machine on, filling the air with a sound Jess knew well.

Once her oxygen levels climbed, the woman's color started coming back. Her eyes blinked open. She gazed up at the ceiling then looked around. Her eyes rounded when she spotted Jess, but when Mary moved up along-side, her face relaxed. "I got sick."

"The smoke, Hassie." Jess's mother took the woman's hand while Jess moved to the opposite side of the bed. "We should have had you on oxygen right away to clear it out. You can't live without lungs, darlin', and if you're going to raise those two sweet babies, oxygen is required. Why didn't you come see me?"

"Or go to the hospital when they suggested it?" Jess asked. When the woman looked up at her, Jess knew why.

It wasn't just the threadbare clothing or the dull hair that told the story. Or the shoes that had seen a lot of miles. It was an air, a posture, between the man and the woman that spoke the truth of the matter. When money's scarce, the hospital is the last place someone wants to be, especially if there's no insurance involved. One hospital stay could ruin an impoverished family.

"I couldn't, Mary. You know that," the old woman whispered. The strain of talking aggravated the hoarseness of her voice, and Jess raised a hand.

"End of conversation for the moment," she told her. "I know my mom's easy to talk to, but your lungs and throat need rest. You've got a fever, not too bad, but enough to tell us we might have pneumonia setting in. You need care right now."

Hassie drew her brows down quickly. "I gotta get back."

"You don't," Mary told her, then addressed the old man who'd followed them through the door. He stood in the shadows, wringing his hands. "Ed, are you working?"

He nodded, and there was no denying the fear in his eyes. "But if Hassie needs me, I can call in."

"We'll keep an eye on her, Ed, if that's all right with you," Mary said. The comfort of her words was deepened by the warm concern in her voice. "We can keep her on oxygen here and we can prescribe what's needed, so all we need is someone to mind the kids. Do you think one of your nieces could do that, Ed? While you go on to work? Ed's got a part-time job at the convenience store up Route 73," she told Jess. "He's got a couple of nieces nearby."

"The girls'll step up. Ma don't like askin' for help." He darted a look of regret at his sick wife. "She's afraid someone will call the county and they'll snatch the little ones away, but Zannah's got two righteous-good daughters. They'll stand by."

"Perfect, Ed." Her mother smiled at him. "Hassie's in the best possible hands here with Jess. Did you know that she's been an ER doc in New York City for years? Now that's a bit of business, let me tell you," she added as she swung open the door.

"I seen how busy it was on the news," he replied as he pulled a too big jacket around his middle. "Folks every which way, and so many lights. Maybe too many," he added before his voice faded as the door swung shut behind him.

Too many lights.

His words would give her something to think about later, but right now she had a patient, an old woman who had no idea how serious her condition might be.

Shane came closer. "Can I help with anything?"

"Shane Stone." The old woman peered up at him through narrowed eyes. "I heard you were back."

"Yes, ma'am."

She frowned at him. Suddenly, Jess felt the need to protect him.

Then Hassie reached out a frail hand. "Folks shoulda stood up for you back then, Shane. All of us. No matter what pushed you to do what you did, we all shoulda been there in that court tellin' that judge what a good boy you were. I'm sorry we didn't do that, and I know Mary's girl is 'bout to make me stop talkin'—"

"Don't make me get a muzzle, ma'am," Jess said in a gentle tone. Sixteen years of emergency medicine had taught her that sometimes the heart needed to heal right along with the body.

"No worries, Miss Hassie." Shane smiled down at the old woman. That smile didn't just warm Jess's heart. It melted a corner that had turned to ice long ago. Maybe enough to let some light back in. "It was a long time back, and I learned right quick how to turn lemons into that lemonade folks like so well. It all turned out fine."

"It didn't."

Something in the old lady's gaze made Jess want to let her go on, but she couldn't.

"I'm sending him on his way so you stop talking, Miss Hassie," she scolded lightly as she rechecked her vitals. "You need rest, and oxygen, and a course of antibiotics. And Shane's got work to do."

Shane took the cue. "Plenty of it. I'll stop back later to see how you're doing, Miss Hassie. Still like those butter rum candies?"

Her face brightened. A stern look from Jess kept her quiet, but she nodded and Shane gave her a thumbs-up.

"I'll see what I can do."

Shane thought he'd been gone long enough from his hometown to prevent any waves of emotion.

*Wrong.*

He hadn't expected Jess to be an issue because she'd

been saving lives in Manhattan, not Kendrick Creek, right? So he hadn't been prepared to find her teetering on the edge of an icy mountain road.

That was his first wake-up call.

Finding out about her battle with cancer?

Definitely a second wave of rough-road emotion.

And seeing Hassie Trembeth lying there sick in the clinic was a firm third. He hadn't gotten to the outlying places in town yet. But he'd been raised on the graveled road up the creek from the Trembeth place.

Shane's mind went back thirty years as he crossed the road to check on the demolition crew.

He used to run errands for the Trembeths. Ed had lost a lung to tuberculosis years before a simple course of pills thwarted the disease, and he got out of breath easy back then.

And they'd lost her their son years back, so there'd been no one left to do the heavy lifting, the yard work, the upkeep on their tiny cabin.

Hassie had sent him cards in prison. She and Mary Bristol had been part of a small group of people who hadn't forgotten him. Those notes and cards had fed his faith and kept him going.

Seeing her lying there, sick and feeble, broke his heart because he hadn't sent her a card in years.

*You've been busy building a business, helping Chrissie, and raising two kids. Cut yourself some slack.*

Yet the guilt rose up and he had a hard time tamping it down.

"Hey, boss, we're set up. You give the nod and we'll bring this one down." Brian Vee, one of his foremen, met him along the road's edge. "Makes it convenient, not having a sidewalk or grass edge to worry about."

His words made Shane look around. He clapped Brian on the back. "That's it."

Brian frowned, confused.

"A sidewalk. Something that ties the businesses into a community setting." He looked left and pointed. "That little parking area could be expanded to give the town a municipal parking lot."

"Except who's going to use it, Shane?" Brian's skeptical expression took in the shabby buildings that hadn't been destroyed by fire.

"Everything starts somewhere, Brian. Why not here? Now? Go ahead with this and the next one. Mary owns both those places, and I'm going to sketch out an idea and present it to the town board and see what they think. Let's start small. But if we get things started, and others jump on board, that's how we get things happening. Like on that street in Baltimore."

"Big city, lots of help. Boss, I hear you, but this is a different situation. Different setting, different population."

Shane disagreed. "They're folks who want the best for their families, same as you and me. We'll figure it out, Bri. I understand the time frame," he added when he noted the hint of worry in the other man's eyes. Brian had a fiancée in Maryland, a woman with two kids. His wedding was slated for late March, scheduled so that it wouldn't interfere with their busy construction season. "I'll have you back home in time for your wedding."

Brian waved that off. "I'm here as long as you need

me, Shane. Kate and I can honeymoon right here if needed. We'll see this through." He strode off. He was a good man. He'd been jailed for a crime he hadn't committed, and Shane understood all the emotions that piggy-backed on that. The only difference was that Shane had done it purposely.

Brian had been with Stonefield for a dozen years and Shane couldn't find a better leader. He wasn't a believer, but Shane had put that on his personal prayer list a long time ago.

He'd added Jess to that list yesterday.

The rest was in God's time, but when he thought of Jess's health battle, he'd increased his prayers exponentially because fighting cancer was tough enough. Fighting it without faith had to be much more difficult. But right now he needed to figure out demo removal and come up with a suitable place to live with two kids. He wasn't sure he could do either with so much closed down for the season.

That just meant he needed to try harder.

# Chapter Six

Jess pulled the curtain a little further around Hassie's bed as the woman drifted into a normal sleep. She went through the door and crossed the small front room to her mother. Concern sparked Mary's gaze as she scanned her phone, but the look disappeared as Jess neared. "Do you think we'll have others with lung damage? Or injuries?"

Mary nodded. "Yes. Several injured people got help immediately, but the Hassies of the world suffer in silence." She jutted her chin toward the back room where Hassie now rested. "In this case, the silence could be lethal. The fire swept in at night, with no warning, while folks were sleeping. We may have only lost three people, but in a town this small, everyone knows those three people, and a good number are related to them. It's the outliers I'm concerned about," she explained. "Folks in damaged trailers and places with no decent plumbing. They've been eking out a living for decades or even generations, but when something like this hits, it hits them hardest."

"Like Hassie?" Jess whispered. The last thing she wanted was to embarrass the sick old woman.

"That woman's got a heart of gold, but they've had their share of trouble," Mary said. "The little ones are their great-grandchildren. They lost their son a long time back to a work-related accident. He was a good man, but his wife remarried a scoundrel.

"Drugs entered the equation. Their granddaughter, Weeza, followed a similar path. Along the way, Weeza had two little ones. When she took off to Florida, Hassie and Ed stepped in with the kids. Weeza overdosed less than a year ago." Mary shook her head. "Sorry. Didn't mean to go on. It makes the whole town sound backward, and it isn't, but every town has its share of sad stories, I expect."

"Every city, too, Mom." Jess put an arm around her mother's shoulders. "You save as many as you can. And it's not that I don't think about the rest, but in a city with nine million people, things get blurred real easy."

"I'd have a hard time with that," Mary admitted on a sigh.

Jess had, too, at first. Then she'd grown more accustomed to it. Now, standing in the converted law offices, she realized that may have been a bad thing.

A knock sounded lightly on the front door before it swung open. "Mary? Jess? Are you in here?"

The familiar voice took Jess back in time. "Devlyn?"

Her old high school friend stepped inside with a

school-age boy. The boy stood there, solemn and still, as if not sure of his place.

"I can't believe it." Jess crossed the room but stopped short when she drew closer. Her friend was wearing a smile, but there was no mistaking the look of grief in her green eyes. Jess took a breath and then hugged her. "It's been almost twenty years, Dev."

"Way too long, Jess. Gosh, we've missed you around here." The sorrow in Devlyn's tone matched the sadness in her eyes. She reached an arm around the boy's shoulders.

Jess took the hint swiftly. "Dev, who's this young man that looks so much like you?"

"You think?" Devlyn smiled, but Jess noted the anxiety behind it. "This is little Jed."

"Named for his grandpa, I expect." Devlyn had been one of her best friends throughout childhood, and Jed McCabe had been good to both girls. He and Devlyn's mother had included Jess in everything, and their house had been like a second home to her. "I'm so sorry he's gone."

"Heaven got a winner when it called Jed McCabe home." Devlyn's voice held all the Southern lyricism Jess had worked so hard to slough off. "Jed, this is my old friend, Jess Bristol. She's Dr. Mary's daughter, and she's a doctor, too. We grew up together."

"Where's her hair?"

Devlyn's mouth dropped open. She went pale then two bright spots of color blushed her cheeks. She started to scold the boy but Jess squatted right down and looked him in the eye. "Gone." She pulled off her colorful cap and showed him. "I got sick," she explained in a calm tone. She might not be accustomed to babies, but once a kid was old enough to ask pertinent questions, she knew how to respond. Quiet honesty tended to win the day with children, whether they were sick, injured, or even dying, and she'd dealt with all three. "The medicine they gave me to make me better made my hair fall out. But look—" she bent her head slightly "—it's growing back now. You can feel it if you want."

He shrunk back then reached out a tentative hand and passed it lightly over her heady. "It's soft," he told her.

"Thank you." She smiled at him, then put her cap back in place. "I wear the hat because it's winter. When you don't have hair, your head gets cold. And nobody wants a cold head. Do they?"

He shook his head. "No. My mom and her friends make stuff so that people don't get cold. Hats and scarves and mittens and blankets and stuff. But they all got burned."

Jess lifted her gaze to Devlyn's. "You lost a lot in the fire?"

"Not the most important thing," Devlyn said firmly. "He's standing right here."

"And as cute as can be," Jess affirmed.

"Devlyn." Mary had gone into the back room to check on Hassie. She crossed the room quickly and gave Devlyn a big hug, then reached into a pocket of her scrub jacket. Withdrawing a pair of candy canes, she held them out to Jed. "Cherry or peppermint?"

"The fruity ones are best," he told her matter-offactly. "Are you working here, Dr. Mary?" He took in the office setting with curious eyes.

"Just until my office gets fixed. It'll take a while, Jed. How are you doing?" she asked the boy.

The boy's eyes welled with tears. He shook his head, and Jess's eyes filled, too. She didn't dare look at Devlyn to see the effect the child's emotions were having on her. "Not too good," he whispered in a choked voice.

"I know." Mary put a hand of comfort on his little shoulder and bent closer. "Life is like that, Jed," she said in a soft, even voice. "Sometimes bad things happen, and it takes us a while to realize that bad things only happen once in a while. Mostly we're surrounded by good things. And it's okay to be sad and even a little worried and scared. We all get like that sometimes. Even grown-ups."

"Even you?" he asked, surprised, as if he couldn't imagine Dr. Mary getting upset.

"Even me," she told him as she unwrapped the candy cane for him. A hint of sadness shadowed her eyes with the admission. "Happens to all of us, I expect."

Hassie coughed in the back room and Mary moved that way. "I'll see to her, Jess. You take some time with Devlyn."

"She's amazing." Devlyn's eyes followed Mary until she disappeared into the two-bed clinic. "Within hours after the fire, she had a cleaning crew in here, getting this ready for an office and a place for folks who needed care. By the end of that day, it was ready. I don't know anyone else like her," Devlyn admitted. "Except maybe you."

"I can't even imagine what would make you say that," Jess replied while Jed seemed to be enjoying his candy cane.

"Working in the city, in the emergency room, with all the busyness and craziness," Devlyn replied. "Things here must seem real backward to you. You stuck it out through all that sickness up there, on top of everything else that happens in a big city."

Jess had been in treatment throughout the recent pandemic, staying distant because her suppressed immune system had put her at a greater risk. She'd hated being unable to help, but she'd had no choice, so she was the last one who should be getting kudos for anything. "I can only hope to be as strong as Mom someday," she told Devlyn honestly, but she couldn't address the truth behind her friend's words.

This *did* seem backward by comparison. Her mother's makeshift office was clean and solid, but it wasn't anything like what she'd find in the city or the suburbs. And yet…

A thought came to Jess as she spotted Shane's work crew beginning demo on one of the burned-out buildings across the street.

Maybe there was a different goodness in all of this. One she hadn't been mature enough to appreciate years ago.

She put an arm around Devlyn's shoulders. "You drink coffee?"

"My blood is part java," her old friend replied.

"Then what do you say to we take a drive and get this office a few necessities?"

"Like bandages and stuff?" Jed asked.

Jess touched his head lightly. "You've got it, dude. Bandages—and a coffee machine. And maybe a mini-fridge, because I might have been in the city for a long time, but the country girl in me loves real cream in her coffee. You game, Devlyn?"

"I'd love it."

"I'll steal Mom's keys," Jess said. "You may not have heard, but my SUV is halfway down the mountain."

"Oh, I heard." Devlyn batted her eyelashes and this time a true smile brightened her face. "Shane Stone to the rescue as he rappelled his way down the mountain to retrieve your things after saving your life in a death-defying act of courage."

Of course, she'd heard. There was no such thing as privacy in Kendrick Creek.

Jess had been fairly anonymous in the city. No one was anonymous here.

She told her mother about their mission, jotted down a short list of things Mary needed, and ten minutes later, she, Devlyn and Jed were in the SUV.

"Where are we headed?" she asked Devlyn.

"Sevierville," Devlyn told her. "Every shop you need is right there." She clicked her seat belt into place as a shadow fell across the driver's window.

Jess looked up, straight into Shane's big blue eyes. Once she looked into his eyes, a part of her didn't want to stop.

She lowered the window and he leaned in slightly. "Heading out?" he asked her easily before shifting his attention. "Hey, Devlyn."

"Hey, Shane."

"Are you really going to fix our house?" Jed asked from the back seat.

Shane nodded. "Could be. That okay with you?"

"Maybe. Will it be bigger?" Jed persisted, and Shane shrugged.

"All stuff we'll sort out. Are you guys on a run for supplies for the emergency clinic space?"

"Yup, plus a coffee maker."

"I will happily be your first customer, Doctor, because there isn't a place left to get a cup of coffee here in town."

"Is that right?" she drawled. Jess hadn't embraced her drawl in a whole lot of years.

"Right as rain." He pointed left. "I parked my office trailer down the road near the church, and that's fine for the guys working nearby. But the town's too spread out to make it convenient for the people working up here. It's too far to go to grab coffee. Every half hour gone is work time we've lost."

"So if I make sure there's coffee at both ends of town?" She offered the leading question purposely and her reward was his smile.

"I'd be downright pleased, ma'am."

Jess blushed. She knew she did, but she ignored it and gave him a quick nod. "I'll make it happen, Shane."

He was about to turn away then didn't. He paused. Held her gaze. And for just a moment, the strength in his eyes held her captive. Then he blinked and backed away. "Sounds good."

* * *

Coffee with Jess.

*Put the brakes on this*, his brain scolded. *You've got a job to do, a family to raise, and over thirty people depend on you for weekly paychecks in Maryland. And in case you haven't noticed, Jess Bristol isn't in any condition to handle a mountain romance with no future. Neither are you, so knock it off.*

Good advice.

He drove back to the work trailer to grab coffee and sketch out an idea for the upcoming town meeting. Pete had just finished brewing a pot and was taking the coffee to the church work crew. He pointed to the computer as Shane moved forward. "I pulled up a list of rental cabins nearby. It gets pricey."

Pete's voice deepened as Shane surveyed the list. "Even if the guys go two to a cabin, we're talking nearly two grand a month for each unit. A lot of them aren't open, bein' New Year's Eve and all, so the logistics are awkward. One of them might cut us a break for booking long-term during the off-season. I'm going to check things out once I drop the coffees off. There're a half dozen of these places a short ride away."

Most of the rental places hadn't existed when Shane had lived here, but the proximity to Pigeon Forge, Gatlinburg and Dollywood had spurred growth. "I knew a couple of owners back in the day. I worked for one while I was a teenager." He pointed to the name on the computer screen. "I lived just up the road from him, Pete."

"Should we approach him first?"

Art Billings had been a decent boss, but he'd been so disappointed with Shane's indictment that he'd broken off all contact. Shane may have come a long way, but he'd never forgotten the look of pure disappointment that had darkened Art's face way back then. He shook his head. "Nah. You go ahead and check out some of the others. I've got an idea for the town meeting that I want to flesh out."

"I'll keep you posted," Pete told him. The metal door clicked shut behind him and the sound of Pete's engine broke the midday quiet.

Shane started a fresh pot of coffee and didn't grab the laptop.

He pulled up several sheets of paper instead.

The process of fleshing out a project by hand helped him visualize what he'd need to get the job done. He'd taught himself how to use the computer programs long ago. A few of the more basic ones he'd learned in prison; he'd expanded his technological proficiency once he was out.

But he always liked to begin the initial process by hand. He poured himself some coffee once it finished burbling. He was about to sit when a knock sounded on the work trailer's door. He set his cup down, crossed the narrow space and opened it. Graham Tyler, an old antagonistic schoolmate, stood in the doorway. He met Shane's gaze then indicated the trailer with a wave of his hand. "Can I come in?"

Part of Shane wanted to refuse. He'd done some side jobs for Graham's parents as a teen. He'd worked for a lot of folks back then, taking any job that would help pad the nonexistent family income. Graham hadn't just treated him like a lowlife on the job, he'd been a jerk to Shane in high school. While that was all a long time ago, Shane wasn't in the frame of mind to walk down memory lane if he wanted his presentation ready.

But the years had softened his attitude, so he pulled the door open against his better judgment. "Yeah, sure."

Graham entered and glanced around. Shane was almost spoiling for the other man to make fun of his work space when Graham surprised him. "You've got a good operation going, Shane." He'd had the hood of his jacket drawn up against the cold. He shoved it back. His hair had thinned, but that wasn't the only thing that had changed. The old look of disdain was gone, too.

Shane motioned to the coffee maker. "Coffee?"

Graham moved that way. "Can I help myself?"

"Cream's alongside."

"Word is, your partner's been checking out rental spots for you and your crew," Graham said as he filled a paper cup with coffee.

Shane nodded.

"I own Creekside Cabins," Graham told him. "My father bought it about twenty years back, and I bought him out when he decided to marry a woman half his age and travel the world."

Shane wanted to feel sorry for him, but Graham's parents had always put on a great show of being "the perfect family," attending church every Wednesday and Sunday. Sitting on the town council. Golfing in the latest country-club fashions even though there wasn't a country club for miles near Kendrick Creek.

Graham had made sure everyone knew he came from privilege. He'd made Shane's last two years of high school awful because Shane hadn't shot hoops or played ball or done anything the rest of the guys considered fun.

He'd worked. He'd worked and he'd helped raise Chrissie. When she'd messed up big-time, he'd known that part of it was on him, but also on the smattering of people who'd treated them like second-class citizens. Graham had been one of those people, and Shane was a little ashamed that the past still stung even after all these years.

"I came by to say I'd like to donate cabins for you and your crew to use while you're here."

"Donate?" Shane didn't cover the doubt in his voice. His time with the Tylers wouldn't have ranked "altruism" on the short list.

"I know what each local place charges in the off-season, and even if they gave you a break, that's a lot of cash or credit we're talking." Graham continued, "I also know you're doing a lot of this renovation on your own dime."

"I don't need charity," Shane said it mildly, but he was firm enough to make his meaning clear.

"I'd say restitution," Graham replied. "I was a jerk when I had no reason to be, to you and your sister. I can't change that," he added, "but I can show the world that I'm not a jerk anymore, and this is one way of doing it. No one uses the cabins in January, and rarely in February, so it's not even all that much of a sacrifice on my part," he continued, as if to lessen the charitable aspect.

"But I have fourteen cabins overlooking the creek and Route 32. Pete said you need eight?"

Graham's admission about the past put the ball in Shane's court because God's word was pretty clear on the whole forgiveness thing. The guy was personally trying to right old wrongs. Not offering forgiveness would put the onus back on Shane because grace was a two-way street. "Eight works."

"That leaves me six to rent out if needed. I know we've got a bad history, Shane." Graham shoved his hands into his pockets and rocked back on his heels, his brow creasing. He didn't sigh, but if ever a guy looked like he was wiping the slate of his soul clean, it was the guy standing in front of him. "And that's my fault. I'd feel a whole lot better about things if you let me do this."

Shane longed to refuse.

He wanted to shrug off Graham's largesse and let him know he could fund his crew, but that would be an expensive way to make an adolescent point.

"I get why you'd say no," Graham acknowledged. "But I'm hoping we're old enough now to put the past behind us. Everybody in town knows you didn't have to do this, and we're all grateful."

Put like that, Shane didn't really have a choice. He'd just read Matthew's retelling of the Sermon on the Mount the night before, and Jesus was clear about one thing: better to take the plank out of your own eye than worry about a speck in your brother's. Was it coincidence that his Bible fell open to Matthew's Gospels last night?

Probably not, considering the application of Christ's

words today. He clenched his jaw slightly then dipped his chin. "It would save us a hunk of money, Graham. I'd be obliged."

"They can move in anytime," Graham told him. "I don't have a housekeeper available right away. Will the guys mind? Zoey Banks normally does the daily cleaning, but her house suffered some damage from the fire. I sent her home with pay so she can put things back together there. She said that Pete told her you'd put her on the list ASAP because she's got two little kids, and that's when I realized what you were doing."

Shane hadn't come to Kendrick Creek looking for recognition. He'd come to offer his own form of payback. "My work up north is slow right now."

"That's a gentleman's answer." Graham reached into his pocket and handed over eight sets of keys. "The cabin number is on the key. Number one is the Wilcox place, the old farmhouse that sits near the road. I did the renovation on it and it's got three bedrooms. My mom calls it a cozier setting than the rustic cabins, but I like the raw wood look myself."

"I'll check that one out myself," Shane told him. "I've got two kids with me. The Wilcox place might be perfect for us."

"You've got kids? That's nice. Real nice." Graham looked like he had more to say, but didn't.

"Chrissie's kids, actually. She passed away a year and a half ago. Her kids are with me now."

Graham's face went taut. He hesitated then shook his head as if to clear it. "I'm sorry, man. I had no idea. That bites."

"Yeah." Shane set the keys on the countertop. "I'll hand these out to the guys. And thank you, Graham."

"None needed. You've given me a way to make amends. That's plenty, right there."

He walked out and Shane took a few seconds to process what just happened.

Having Graham Tyler come by to ask forgiveness and offer free lodging for a couple of months would have been the last thing he'd have expected.

And yet that's what had happened.

He pulled out his chair to get back to work but studied the small pile of keys for a few drawn-out seconds.

Second chances.

He'd had a share of those since going to prison, and he'd worked hard to make the most of them. But this gesture took him by surprise because maybe—just maybe—Kendrick Creek had turned into an even better version of itself while he'd been gone.

## Chapter Seven

Shane had lost count of how much coffee he'd consumed that day, which gave him the perfect excuse to grab another. He'd finish the town specs later. Right now he wanted to see the cabin, call Nettie and have her bring the kids into town. He'd deliberately kept them out of the fire areas, but with school starting in a couple of days, he needed to get things in order. If he could settle the kids here, they wouldn't have New Year's Eve and New Year's Day in a roadside motel.

Jess texted him as he pulled into Creekside Cabins. Double-checking before we leave the store because I know there aren't a lot of shopping options close to town. Anything you need?

There was, actually, if he wanted to get the kids settled here today. He texted back quickly. Give me five?

She sent him a thumbs-up emoji.

The drive forked in front of the modest farmhouse on his right. The two-lane driveway continued to a series of uphill wood-sided cabins while a narrower driveway led to the clapboard-sided rental. He climbed out of the truck, went up the sturdy steps onto a well-built porch, unlocked the door and went in.

The interior was pleasant. Graham had done a decent job on the reno. Not fancy, and not tricked out, but everything was solid and clean. He checked around, then texted Jess back quickly. Kitchen towels. Bath towels. Bedsheets. And kid-friendly soap. Graham Tyler offered his cabins, but we didn't bring anything like this along and there is nothing here.

How many cabins?

Was she really going to shop for all eight? Suddenly, his phone rang and Jess's number flashed in the display. He answered quickly. "Listen, I didn't mean to hijack your shopping trip—"

"Don't waste time arguing." Her reply was crisp and to the point. Typical Jess. That much hadn't changed. "I'm in the store with Devlyn and Jed. Unless you suddenly have time to do this?"

He sure didn't. "I don't."

"Then tell me. Do the beds have pillows?"

"Yes."

"Blankets?"

"Yes. But no sheets. Three double beds in the house. Not sure about the other cabins yet."

"Devlyn says there are double beds in all the cabins. So sheets and towels for them all?"

The money he'd save would more than cover the linen expenses. "Yes, please."

"Anything else?"

"Well…" He hesitated, but she was in the heart of the shopping district. "It's New Year's Eve and I don't have anything here to make it special. We always try to do something fun."

"I have no idea what that means."

He hadn't either until he started helping Chrissie. "Chicken nuggets. Mozzarella sticks and marinara. Cupcakes or something like that. The kind of stuff we wouldn't eat every day. And soda."

"Sounds like a perfect evening. I'll have Devlyn guide me. Can you do laundry there?"

"Yes. In the house I'm in."

"I'll grab you some laundry soap, too. What about coffee makers?"

Duh. Yes, a coffee machine graced the kitchen counter. "It has one. Yes."

"I'll grab coffee for each cabin, then. And cups. Gotta start the day right."

"I concur."

She didn't laugh but he thought he read a smile in her tone. "I'll let Mom know that I'll be a little longer than expected. I'll text you when we're on our way back, okay?"

"Yeah. And, Jess?"

"Hmm?"

He pictured her face, the way she'd arch that left eyebrow in question, the curve of her cheek, how her hair used to cascade over her shoulders and down her back. She'd been a girl back then. She was all woman now. "Thanks."

Her tone tipped up. "No problem."

Nearly ninety minutes later, Mary called as Jess was approaching the Creekside Cabin area. "Hey, Mom. I can take the overnight watch for Hassie. I'm just about to drop off the stuff Shane needs for the cabins they'll be staying in. Then I'll—"

"I'm home," Mary told her.

Jess paused, surprised because she'd expected her mother to be at the temporary office.

"I've got Jenny Billings with Hassie for the evening, then Marta Lacey is going to stay the night," Mary explained.

"You sure?" Jess asked. "I don't mind staying there. Won't be the first all-nighter I've pulled."

"Folks here like to look after their own," Mary told her, and she sounded a touch tired as she said it. "They've known Hassie for years. Jenny's a practical nurse and Marta's an RN with my practice."

"I didn't realize that." Another stab of guilt hit her. Her mother had frequently inquired about Jess's job, her patient load and her long days. But when was the last time Jess had asked for information about Kendrick Creek Medical?

She couldn't remember. "Okay, I'll see you shortly, then. I'm pulling into Creekside right now."

"Sounds good."

The call disconnected as she parked next to a gray sedan with Maryland plates just as Shane parked his truck behind her. He climbed out. "Perfect timing." He rounded the truck and came her way. "You dropped Devlyn off?"

"Yes. We had a nice time shopping together, though. I've missed her." Admitting that felt odd because it wasn't like she'd even thought about her old friend all that much during all those years away, but today had been nice. Really nice. She opened the back door of her mother's SUV and Shane let out a long, low whistle.

"That's a lot of sheets, Jess."

She hoisted a bag and headed for the door. "Towels are in the back." She clicked the key fob and the back hatch swung up easily. "Do you want everything here or in the cabins?"

"Here's good." He grabbed two bags of towels and met her at the steps, then swung open the door. "Hey, Sam? Jolie?" he called out. "What do you think of the place?"

A super cute boy about Jed's age raced their way then slid in sock-clad feet across the hardwood floor. "So awesome! Did you know there are bears in the woods behind us? Real ones! And they haven't eaten a person in a long, long time. I know because Nettie looked it up on her phone. And the bears didn't get all burned up because they know how to run from fire. And did you know there hasn't been a fire here in a *very long time*?" He slid to a stop, whirled about, then spotted Jess.

He stopped. Stared. His eyes darted from her chemo cap to her face, then back. He swallowed hard.

"Sam, this is Dr. Jess. She's come to town to help, too."

It took Sam a few seconds to gather himself before

he nodded politely. "Hi." He glanced up again, took in the cap and lack of hair, then quickly shoved his feet into a pair of boots tucked against the inside wall. "Is there more stuff to get?"

Shane nodded and the boy grabbed a hoodie off the row of hooks. "I'll help. You can stay inside," he told Jess, and his tender voice showed concern.

"Thanks, Sam."

Shane met her gaze, but he kept his thoughts quiet. It was clear that the boy was trying to spare Jess. Because she was a woman? Or because of the cancer?

Sammy darted one more quick look to her head then dashed outside.

*Definitely cancer.*

Shane followed him out.

That left Jess cooling her heels inside, not used to being left behind. She was just about to charge out the front door to show them that she was perfectly capable of taking care of herself when footsteps clattered down from upstairs. She turned and came face-to-face with a girl. Her presence startled the girl, who drew to a stop and frowned.

Jess moved forward. "You must be Chrissie's daughter."

The frown didn't disappear, but the shoulders relaxed. "How do you know that?"

"You look like her," said Jess.

The girl's eyes went wide. "You knew my mother?"

"Yes." Jess stuck out her hand. "Hi, I'm Jess Bristol. I came down to help the town, too." It sounded odd, saying it like that, but it sounded good, because maybe she hadn't just come down to help her mother.

"You know Pops?"

"Your uncle?" Jess asked. When the girl nodded, Jess smiled. "We didn't call him Pops, but yes. I knew him. He was a hard worker then, and he's a hard worker now."

Footfalls thundered across the front porch before Shane and Sam thrust open the door.

"More sheets!" Sam sang out.

"And you can never have too many towels," Shane noted as he handed off bags to Jess. "If you take these, I won't track up the floor."

"Sure." She motioned to the girl. "How about if you and I sort out the sheets and towels for each cabin? Then, when they stop by, you only have to hand them a bag?"

The girl hesitated.

"That would be a nice help, Jolie." Shane offered the encouragement from the door.

She didn't move right away, but when she did, she moved with purpose. "Okay." She opened a bag and began setting wrapped sets of sheets around the room. "We can organize it first, then bag them."

"Excellent." Jess took her cue from the girl and began laying out more packaged sheets. "How many men are we talking?"

"Thirteen, counting Pete," said Shane. He headed out the door once more. "Thanks, ladies."

Jolie didn't reply. She emptied the bags with quick hands, then frowned. "They don't all match."

"We pretty much wiped out three displays of double-size sheets," Jess admitted. "I don't think the men will care, do you?"

Jolie studied her for a moment then shrugged. "But we want it nice, don't we? As nice as we can make it?"

The set of her chin. The shadow in her eyes. The almost helpless look she swept around the somewhat bare-bones living room, as if she couldn't believe she was there. Or maybe she wasn't happy anywhere.

Jess tucked that thought aside until she had time with Shane alone. "You're absolutely right, so let's match them up as best we can, okay?" She indicated the bags stuffed with big cotton towels in a variety of colors. "Ready?"

Jolie's expression brightened. "All right." She took over with quick, sure hands. "I like blues and yellows together, even though everyone tends to put greens with blues." She tucked towel groupings on top of sheets as she spoke. "And blue and orange is fun, isn't it?"

When she put the melon-shaded towels with a powder blue set of sheets, Jess didn't hide her surprise. "I would have never done that, but it looks great. What made you think of that?"

Jolie pointed to a window. "God."

Jess frowned.

"When you look at nature, you see all the colors and how they mix and match," the girl explained, but she didn't stop to talk. She kept working, and each decision about coordinating the hodge-podge of colors seemed to please her. "Like a sunrise over the bay. Pops rents a boat sometimes so we can go out fishing, and the colors make me smile. Because even if they're different, somehow they belong together."

Shane and Sam came in again and dropped off more bags. Jess didn't miss Shane's look of approval as he noticed Jolie's efforts, almost as if her calm inspired his. They went back out and by the time they brought in the remaining supplies, Jolie had filled the room with a rainbow of linens.

"Let's put a can of coffee with each set," noted Jess. "And a bag of cups for each cabin, okay?"

"You thought of all this?" Jolie looked at her again and this time seemed to see Jess, but she didn't seem dissuaded by the chemo hat or thinned eyebrows.

"Well, your dad needed help and we didn't have a lot of patients to look after at the clinic, so I made a shopping run. It worked out. The way things have a way of doing most times."

"Do they?" Jolie looked unconvinced, but changed her expression when Shane turned toward them from hanging up his jacket on the nearby hooks.

He saw it, though.

From Jess's perspective, she could see the girl's pain and the uncle's reflection of it, and her heart went tight in her chest.

Then Sam kicked his boots off in the general area of the mat and rushed their way. "I can put stuff in bags, Jolie."

"The way they're supposed to go? Or just shoving everything together like you usually do?" she asked, but the disapproval in her tone didn't seem to affect the boy.

"I don't think Fred and Giz and Whistler and the

other guys care about that stuff," Sam said practically. "They just want to relax when they're done working. Like Pops."

"Do you want help?" Shane directed the question at Jolie.

She didn't meet his gaze.

Eyes averted, she studied her carefully laid out piles and Jess read the girl's conundrum. She'd made an effort, and in her ten-year-old eyes, that effort meant something. Jess perched on the arm of a chair and offered an option. "How about if Jolie and I put the bags together and Sam hands them out when the guys come along?"

Glimmers of light flashed beyond the windows as each cabin's dusk-to-dawn lights came to life. The lights didn't just brighten the campgrounds, they brightened Jolie. She aimed a look of surprising patience at her brother and smiled. "He can help."

"Yes!" Sam fist-pumped the air with boyish gusto. "And I won't mess up your colors, okay?"

"Good." They worked together and, as Jess stood to go, a woman padded down the stairs behind her. Spotting Jess, she smiled broadly.

"I knew I heard a new voice, but I was organizing the kids' things and wanted to get that done before I head north."

"Nettie, this is Jess Bristol," offered Shane. "Jess, this is Nettie, our wonderful friend and nanny."

"Although some of us are old enough to not need a nanny," muttered Jolie, but she gave the older woman a genuine smile, one that touched her eyes. "Nettie and I are just really good friends."

Nettie laughed and crossed the room to hug both kids. "I get to be the bossier friend, however," she reminded the girl. "But you are growing up, Jolie. And it's a pleasure to see it." She turned to Shane. "If I can get four hours of driving in today, I can be back in Baltimore by midday tomorrow," she told him. "They're going to induce my daughter," she explained to Jess. "Just got the news this afternoon. I must be there to welcome the first Smith-Garcia into the world."

"You'll drive safe?" asked Shane.

The older woman grabbed him into a hug. "I will be safe, and so will you. All of you. And I can't wait to see pictures of the transformation, Jolie. You promise to send them?"

"I will." Jolie slipped another set of supplies into one of the big empty bags, then paused and faced Nettie, concerned. "Do you think it will be pretty when it's done, Nettie? For real?"

Shane cleared his throat, pretending insult, but Jess saw the deeper question in the girl's words. She was a worrier who'd lost her mother, had a pesky little brother and had been uprooted from her home and friends. Truth be told, January weather mixed with a fire wasn't an attractive blend. A town filled with dank, wet, icy, smoky-smelling buildings wasn't very inspirational. "You know, I came down that mountain yesterday and I saw the town and I felt like my heart turned into a solid rock," she told Jolie and Sam.

Sam scoffed instantly. "Hearts don't turn into rocks,

silly. I thought you were a real doctor?" he asked, as if amazed that a real doctor would think such a thing.

"I mean I felt bad, seeing it," she explained. "Because I know how beautiful this all is normally. The mountains, the trees, the rolling hills and meadows… The old buildings… The farms and the cows and sheep folks raise… So I felt bad coming down the mountain and seeing all the damage. But then, when I realized your dad—"

Jolie's eyes shot up. She stared at Jess then at Shane as if in challenge.

"—was here to help rebuild things," Jess went on as if she hadn't noticed the girl's reaction, "I saw the hope again. My mom is the doctor here. We'll work to make people well. Shane and the crews are here to rebuild what was lost. And that's a pretty special thing." She turned to Shane. "I'm going to let you guys say your goodbyes," she told him, glancing at Nettie. "Mom's home and I want to touch base with her about the clinic tomorrow because I know we've got a lot of appointments."

"I'll walk you out."

She pulled her coat into place and opened the door. "Good meeting you, Jolie, Sam. Happy New Year."

Sam was busily feeding now unfolded towels into a bag. "Same to you!" Smiling wide, he gave her a little-boy salute.

"Thank you." The gravity in Jolie's voice wasn't lost on Jess. She understood it all too well.

"You're welcome."

Shane followed her to Mary's SUV and shoved his

hands into his pockets. "Do you think I'm crazy for bringing them down here? For doing this in the middle of the school year? I know stuff looks bad now, but I also know that seeing the transformation can be good for kids."

"Are we talking outgoing Sam or reticent Jolie?" she asked directly. "That's the problem with two kids. They're not generally from the same mold."

"That's for sure. And how do you balance that with their loss? With change? With anything?" he asked. "I've been trying to break through Jolie's walls since we lost her mom, and nothing seems to work. It's as if she's spending her life watching. Waiting. Wondering when Chrissie will come back, even though she knows she can't."

Grief and concern vied for control of his voice.

Jess put a hand on his shoulder and met his gaze. "Time, Shane. Not your time line or mine. Hers. It seems like a long time to us, but to a kid, who knows? Keep loving her. Teasing her. And give her time to heal."

"But what if I'm doing it wrong?" Something in his voice touched her.

"There isn't one right way to raise kids, is there? Not like I'm an expert or anything."

He breathed deep then nodded. "I turn it over to God every day, I remember the sparrows that He cares for and all the words of wisdom, but then I see the yearning in Jolie's eyes and I want to fix it."

"Because you're a fixer. But not everything can be

hammered into place," she reminded him. "Some things just fall in line as time goes on."

He met her eyes with his and then reached up a hand to cover hers. "I'm glad you're here, Jess."

Her heart fluttered.

Shane squeezed her hand lightly.

She stepped back.

They had lives to get back to eventually, and his kids had already lost a mother to cancer. No way was she going to risk developing a relationship that might make things worse. "See you tomorrow. Is Devlyn coming over first thing?"

"Sure is. With Jed. The guys wanted to work even with the holiday, and this gives the kids someone to know. Although I'm staying here with them. Can't leave them alone all day."

"That's perfect. It will keep Devlyn busy and give Jed someone to play with."

"Exactly. Good night, Jess. And thanks again."

"You're welcome." She didn't think about his hand over hers or the way their eyes had met and held. She couldn't. And she wasn't about to fall in line with his platitudes about faith, but there was no denying he took comfort in his beliefs.

As did her mother.

While that was fine for them, she'd err on the side of science and facts, every time.

## Chapter Eight

Two days later, Hidey Jones stumbled into the office, looking pretty wasted for one o'clock in the afternoon. Fortunately, their last morning patient had just left and other than Hassie resting in the back, the office was empty except for Mary and Jess.

Distaste made Jess's mouth go sour.

She hated drunkenness. She hated it, and while she'd been able to deal with it in the city's emergency rooms, it was a double punch down here. Maybe because her mother's blood alcohol level had been a soaring midday 0.13% when she'd crashed her car on that mountain road over forty years before with an unsecured child in the back seat. Car seats weren't a rule back then. Jess knew that. But what if her biological mother had cared enough to try and keep her safe? Would she have suffered so many injuries?

"Mary here?" Eyes narrowed, Hidey peered at Jess as if trying to make sense of her.

Mary came out from the back just then, looked at

Hidey and frowned. Jess expected to hear a scolding, but her mother just took the middle-aged man's arm. "Whatever's happened, Hidey, I just want you to know I'm sorry." The comfort and concern in her mother's voice surprised Jess because Mary wasn't one to tolerate stupid behavior. With a light hand on the man's arm, she led him toward the back and the second partitioned area near Hassie. "Real sorry. How about you get a rest here and we can talk about it later, okay?"

"Restin' won't help a thing, Mary. Not one thing. Talkin' won't, either, not when it's gone." He met her gaze with watery eyes and sniffled loudly. "All gone."

"It may keep your wife from doing you bodily harm, Alistair, and that's a start, now, isn't it?"

The use of his given name brought his chin up, or maybe it was the thought of his wife. Jess hadn't even known he had a wife. Who would marry him? She moved to the door. Her mother was handling the situation, but Jess figured brisk, fresh air might keep her from saying something stupid. She reached for the handle just as Shane pushed it open from the other side.

She stepped back.

He came in as her mother returned from tucking the inebriated man in.

"Did Hidey get here all right?" Shane asked.

"*You* sent him?" Jess asked. She didn't even try to mask her feelings.

"He needed help," said Shane quietly.

"He's needed help for a long time," Jess replied.

"He's a patient, Jess," Mary reminded her. "Like any other."

"A drunken one."

Shane frowned. "You're wrong about this, Jess. Hidey hasn't had a drink in over twenty years. I know because he and I had a long chat when I was looking over his property my first day here."

Twenty years?

She looked from him to her mother, surprised. "He was this way when I left, and this way when I came back, so—"

Mary didn't let her finish. "So you assumed he's been that way throughout. Yet he's run a barbecue pit up the road for travelers and locals and has done well with it. He and Merriweather have two great kids, one of whom is playing basketball for the Volunteers."

The Tennessee Volunteers were the University of Tennessee's Division One sports teams.

"And the younger one leads Bible studies for local teens," Mary continued. "Merriweather saw him through a tough time when Alistair lost his son from his first marriage, and she's stood by his side all this time. You've been gone a long time, Jess."

She had.

She knew that.

Worse, she'd disassociated with people here by keeping her distance and not even asking about them. "I didn't know. I'm sorry."

"Apologies don't fix the hurt caused by the expression I saw on your face when I came through a few minutes ago." Her mother wasn't pulling any punches. "Jess, if you're going to work here, you've got to treat people with respect. Everyone."

A part of Jess wanted to argue, but her mother was correct. And Shane was right, too. She'd made an assumption based on old news, and a good ER doctor couldn't afford to do that. She took a deep breath and reached for the door. "You're both right, and I'm pretty ashamed of myself at the moment."

Shane started to say something, but she held up a hand. "I'm going to grab a little time alone. Okay?"

He hesitated then nodded.

So did her mother.

Jess closed the door quietly.

Part of her wanted to slam it, but not at Shane and her mother. At herself because she'd acted foolishly. When she'd read her mother's disappointment and Shane's expression, she'd realized she needed to do better. And that was entirely up to her.

"She'll be all right, Shane."

Shane watched from inside as Jess trudged up the road, chin tucked against the cold, damp day. "You think?"

"I know," Mary replied firmly. "She's got to reason it out herself. Always did. Probably always will. But I can't have her thinking ill of people here. There's a lot of good folks who do all right with less book learning and more hands-on skills."

Shane understood that concept well. "You're talking to one of them. I know you're right, yet I don't want to see her hurting. Cancer does enough of that." He crossed to the front desk, his eyes straying to the lone figure walking away. It took every ounce of willpower not to chase her down to try to make things all right.

But he'd been down this road before, with Chrissie. It was hard for people with no faith to understand the peace and hope that came with believing. He'd learned the hard way that he couldn't force someone toward God. He could only hang out nearby as a living example, hoping they'd find their own way. Chrissie had, eventually, but Jess had always been fiercely independent. No help from God necessary.

He turned back to Mary, knowing there was little he dared do to help Jess. Keeping his feelings in check was hard. It would be much harder if he thought too much about it. Time to refocus on what he could change, which was the brick-and-mortar section of the town.

He held up a sheaf of papers, then laid them out for her to examine. "Sidewalks," he told her, hooking a thumb to the road outside the front window.

Mary Bristol knit her brow.

"On both sides of the street here in town," he continued. "If we create sidewalks along the road, with room for streetlights, we give Kendrick Creek a sense of community. We geographically link things together. I wanted your thoughts before I talk at the town meeting. I put myself on the agenda."

"Whoa." Mary gave a long, low whistle. "This is some major stuff, Shane."

"It looks major," he agreed, "but it's not as extensive as it appears. We've got five Main Street lots that are going to be emptied once demo is done, and that opens a window of opportunity. If we can create a small-town feel along this stretch of road, we draw visitors down from the mountains in greater numbers, which means we can extend the business district and create the town center folks have talked about for years."

Mary had looked doubtful, but the moment he'd laid out the logistics, her expression opened. "That's been a dream of Hidey's ever since he started smoking meat in his front yard. He was so excited when he went to two smokers and his converted truck, but there was never the means to really get it going. Miles Conrad has always tried to thwart this idea. He still thinks they're going to put a highway spur through the valley and that he's sitting pretty on his acreage, so he's led the rallying cry against improving the business district."

"Well, that's selfish and shortsighted, 'cause you know folks love good barbecue," Shane confirmed. "Just the smell of it will coax people off the road, especially if there's a place to park and wander. I'd like to help make this happen, Mary." He pointed to the specs. "I'm only talking a block long on either side and the municipal lot here, but if we give it a start, folks will continue," he reasoned.

"It didn't work when they came up with the idea a quarter century ago, Shane," she reminded him. "When we were raising funds to start renovating the town after the creek washed that little bridge out. I hate to bring that up," she finished apologetically. "I know that started an awful chain of events for you."

Shane had no desire to unbury the past, either. One of those events had put him in jail. "That was then. This is now. But there might be some folks who won't like my involvement, so I'd like your support. Your word goes a long way in this town, Mary."

"You know you've got it, Shane." She held his gaze and, for a moment, he thought she wanted to say more, but she didn't.

"If we build up this stretch—" he pointed to the second and third sketches "—folks could stop here, shop and eat. It's hard to find supper seating at any of the popular places along the parkway, they're so over-crowded. So we take care of them here, then they go on to Pigeon Forge or Gatlinburg or Dollywood. We build businesses, the tourists get a restful place to relax, and everyone wins. And it would ease some of the traffic in those other localities," he added.

"Shane, I love it," she told him outright. "And I'd love to have you talk to Jordan Ash."

"Because?"

"She ran the Dollar Friendly until it burned, but she's always had her eye on the old hardware store to open as a general store. She's told me often enough, and she knows I'd rent it to her, but she hasn't been able to get financing. If banks saw this—" she tapped a finger to his sketches "—they'd rethink her proposal because being a drive-through town has always been a problem. If folks had a reason to stop—"

"The core businesses would draw folks in, and others would come along. Then—"

"Then…" Mary's eyes shone with a glimmer of hope. "We'd have a town."

# Chapter Nine

Jess crossed the quiet road to her mother's damaged clinic building and surveyed it from outside, arms folded across her chest.

The afternoon sun was melting the dirty icicles that had formed during the fire's aftermath. The bright warmth fouled the air with bitter smells.

Almost a third of the town had suffered deep losses, and in a town of less than five thousand, that was a gut-punch. But as she moved back to survey the wrecking crew and the street, something stirred within her.

Her first job had been in Lower Manhattan. She'd walked through the slowly renovated area of the Twin Towers for several years before moving uptown.

If New York City could turn tragedy into beauty, why not Kendrick Creek? Why not Shane and her mother?

*Why not you? Have you got something better to do?*

Instead of looking at the downside of all that had happened this past year, maybe it was time for Jess to start reinventing her life. Starting here. Starting now.

The office door opened across the way. Shane was coming out, with Hidey.

Jess crossed the road deliberately. When she drew close, she stuck out her hand. "Mr. Jones? It's Jess, Mary's daughter. Good to see you, sir."

Shane's brow lifted slightly, but she didn't look his way. She gazed into the sorrowed man's deep gray eyes and spoke truth. "I came home looking forward to your barbecue, Mr. Jones. I've had barbecue lots of places, but nothing as good as yours has been when I've come back to visit. I don't know if it's the mountain wood or the secret sauce or the cuts of meat, but I can honestly say I'll be excited to see you get started again, and if there's anything I can do to help that, I'd be glad to pitch in."

"Miss Jess, you're a doctor. Like your mom."

"Doctors like to eat, too," she assured him. When he smiled—when a gleam of hope brightened those bloodshot eyes—a different warmth went through her.

"I'm in a conundrum right now," Hidey told her. "Everything's gone."

"But I've got a welder in my group here," said Shane. "If we find the right materials, we can design a new smoker or two, right, Hidey? Especially if we can use that old metal shed sitting vacant up the road."

"I don't expect Milt will care," Hidey told him. Milt Smith owned the property he was referencing. "We go way back."

"You ask him and we'll see what they've got in the scrapyard up Route 32," said Shane. "I expect an old oil tank—"

"Just the ticket," declared Hidey. "With a lid that closes up and down. And a damper."

"You sketch out your idea, and we'll see what's available tomorrow. You good for a ride up the road?" Shane asked.

Hidey's smile seemed to grow along with his confidence. "I am." He bobbed his head slightly. "Around nine or so? That's when they open."

"Nine's good."

"I'll be ready." He walked up the sorry-looking road, his head higher than when he'd walked out the door.

Jess followed him with her eyes. "We've got to help him."

She withdrew her phone as she began walking the rest of the affected street. "How bad is it west of here?"

Shane indicated the scorched area marring the mountainside behind them, then the rest of the valley. "It swept in on an east wind, so this all took a direct hit, but once it crossed the valley, the shifting winds bounced it, so the damage is scattered. Some places are a total loss like these. Some are barely touched. And some are bad enough that the owners might not be able to rebuild. Kendall Mills Road is one of those places."

Devlyn's road.

Jess came to Kendrick Creek intent on helping her mother.

Now she wanted to offer help wherever it was needed. "I want to help." She faced him directly. "I'm between positions right now, my time is my own. And I'm not exactly broke, so how can I help? What can I do?" She put a hand on his arm and broached the topic they'd been carefully avoiding since he'd saved her life. "I know you probably hate me for what happened when we were in school, but if you can forgive me and work with me, I think that would be good, Shane. Not just for the town, but maybe—" She held his gaze a little longer than she should have. "For us, too. Because I've spent twenty-five years wishing I'd never run back for my purse that day. If I'd just left it in the trailer overnight, things might have turned out differently. I can't change what happened then," she added sincerely, "but I'm here to help now."

Things sure would have been different.

He'd have put the stolen money back where it belonged and gone on with his life. No one would have known anything, except him and Chrissie. And the nefarious gang in Newport that had put her up to the theft.

But that wasn't what happened. "It's old news, Jess."

"Still. I'm sorry."

She'd done what any responsible citizen should have done, and reported what she'd seen—enough to earn him five years in prison.

He'd survived his time behind bars. Chrissie wouldn't have been so fortunate. In the end, it had all worked out, but he wasn't about to sully Jolie's and Sam's lives with the truth about their mother. But he couldn't shrug Jess off, either. "You really want to help?"

His words didn't seem to satisfy her, but she nodded. "Yes."

"Help raise awareness. Kendrick Creek is small. It doesn't get big press when something like this happens."

"Social media?"

"Any media that shares news or human-interest stories."

"Like Hidey's."

"Except you can't call folks out as if they're begging for help," he reminded her. "That wouldn't work down here."

"Mountain pride."

"And mountain strong," he replied. "I'm heading up the road. Want a lift home?"

"Sure thing. Devlyn's going to bring the kids over so we can look at her options and the kids can play with all my old stuff downstairs. She said Jed and Sam are becoming fast friends, but Jolie could use some girl talk, and since I'm a girl…" She winked, and it took a minute for him to clear his head because Jess wasn't just a girl. She was an amazing and beautiful woman—and absolutely off limits. He rounded the hood, wishing he'd taken time to clean out the truck cab from the past few days, but he'd done everything on the run since the day after Christmas. That included one night of sleeping in the truck when the little motel was short a room because of holiday travelers. The guys and the kids got motel rooms. He took the truck cab. It all worked out.

Jess opened the front passenger door. She stopped. Stared. Then shifted a smile his way, and he wished the smile didn't tug at him like it did. "Fancy quarters, Shane."

He scrubbed a hand to the nape of his neck. "I wasn't expecting anybody to be riding shotgun except Pete, and he's as bad as I am."

"You boys have been bachelors for way too long then," noted Jess. She climbed in, lifted a bag from the floor and started throwing things away.

"Jess, you don't have to do that," he protested from his side, but she kept right on.

"You drive, I'll clean up, and we'll all be happier for the lack of stuff beneath our feet. Deal?"

He couldn't very well stop her, so he shifted the truck into gear and smiled her way. "Shifting is definitely easier with the debris field cleared."

She laughed.

When he drove up to her mother's place less than five minutes later, the truck looked a lot better. "Thank you for the ride," she told him as she opened the door. "I'm going to get rid of this stuff and chat some things up with Devlyn. Or at least give her a shoulder to lean on."

He wanted to join the conversation but he'd already injected enough of his ideas into place. Pushy didn't work well in Tennessee. He gave her a casual two-finger salute. "See you tomorrow."

"Will do." She swung up the short drive with the same stride he'd admired long ago.

A sudden tap on the window brought him back to the present. Devlyn stood there, staring at him. He rolled the window down. "Dev?"

She looked from him to Doc's house and back again. "Opportunities don't come around every day, Shane Stone. They're a hit-and-miss commodity. It does one well to know that."

The kids were still in her car, peering at something in a book. "I've got a lot of stuff on my plate right now,

Devlyn." He didn't smile, but he didn't scold, either. "And a wise man learns to put first things first if he's on the right road. And I am now. So let's leave it, all right?"

"Shane."

He'd dropped his gaze, but met her eyes again. Devlyn's kind heart showed in every facet of her personality and today compassion softened her gaze. "You've always been on the right road."

Her words didn't just put a pause on his heart. They stopped it dead.

"There's a few that know that, Shane," she went on softly while the kids pored over whatever they were reading in the van behind her. "Teenagers are guilty of one thing, my friend. They talk. And if this is your secret to keep, I respect that, but you're back home now, and there are several folks who wish things had happened differently. That they'd spoken up back then. Just so you know."

"Don't know what you're talking about, Dev." He kept his tone smooth and easy, as if she hadn't just rocked his world.

Empathy showed in her eyes. She made a little face of sadness before she accepted his words. "All right, Shane. We play it your way. But just so y'all know, I think the world of you. Thank you for coming back to help." She gave him a short wave as the kids scrambled out of the car and headed to Mary's wood-shingled home.

She knew the truth. It was there in her words, in her gaze.

Others knew, too?

And there were Jolie and Sam, playing with Devlyn's son just a few feet away from him.

He breathed deep.

That usually helped.

Not today.

It only made the adrenaline rush of realization spread farther, because if Devlyn was right, then his past wasn't the well-kept secret he believed it to be.

And that wasn't something he'd bargained for when he'd brought his company—and the kids—south.

## Chapter Ten

Jess gazed down at Jolie's intricate artwork an hour later and sighed. "Honey, that's beautiful. How did you learn to use brushstrokes like that?" Jolie had created a garden of flowers along the base of a medium-size poster board Devlyn had brought along. Through the spectrum of colors, a visual rainbow poured through. Her clever use of words—"In a world of rainbows, you are every color I'll ever need"—and staging, were far beyond any ten-year-old Jess had ever known.

"I just know how. And you have to have the right brushes," she explained.

"Wow." Jess slid a glass of iced tea across the table to Devlyn. Her motion made Jolie jump to pull her work back.

"You should never have liquids near art," she scolded, and Jess paused to give her a straight-on look.

"All right, then. I'll put the glass on the counter. What about you, Jolie? Would you like iced tea with me and Devlyn?"

Jolie glanced from one to the other. "It's okay if I do?"

"Well, it's tea, so yes." Jess gave her a teasing look. "I do believe that tea is an acceptable beverage at age ten. Devlyn, correct me if I'm wrong. Oh…" She paused when a thought came to her. "Will your dad object?"

She got that dark expression again, as if Jess had said something wrong. Very wrong. Then Jolie waved it off. "Pops won't mind. Nettie had rules about caffeine, but Pops said he drank coffee since he was a kid and he's doing all right."

Shane.

It was all Jess could do to keep thoughts of him at bay. She poured a glass of iced tea for Jolie while the boys assembled an array of Sam's toy soldiers in the finished basement. The noise of their battle play made her glad the lower level existed.

"I love iced tea," Jolie told them as she sipped. "I don't know why Nettie wouldn't let us have it."

"I'm sure she only wanted what was best for you," Jess said. "Being a nanny is a major responsibility."

"And we love her." Jolie had moved her painting to a side table. Now she set her glass down. "She's nice to everyone. And she lived with us, so when Pops was late, it was all right. And she liked science, like me, so we could talk about things."

"A live-in nanny is a marvelous thing." Devlyn smiled at Jolie.

"I guess." Jolie studied her tea. "I don't think she's coming back. Ever. Now that her grandson is born."

Jess took a seat and frowned. "What makes you say that?"

Jolie shrugged, pensive. "Her daughter came to our house one night when Pops was at a meeting. It was kind of late. She said that Nettie should be loyal to her own family first, and that she needed her to watch the baby after it got born. I couldn't fall asleep, it was so close to Christmas and... I don't know..." She trailed her finger across the cold glass. "I kept thinking about things and then I heard her daughter's voice, so I listened. She was angry with Nettie. And I heard Nettie crying later, so that wasn't good."

"I'm sorry you heard all that." Jess leaned forward but didn't reach out a hand of comfort. Jolie seemed more comfortable with distance. "Grown-ups get stupid sometimes. We say things we shouldn't and we forget to treat the people we love with respect."

"You don't do that. You're a doctor," Jolie observed. "Every doctor I go to is really nice."

"Even I'm a jerk sometimes, and then I'm ashamed of myself," Jess replied. "Does your dad know about this?"

Jolie's lips went tight, and Jess had a light-bulb moment.

She didn't like Shane being referred to as "her dad."

"Pops" was all right, but each time Jess had called Shane her father or dad, the girl got uptight.

"I didn't tell him. I was hoping I was wrong or that Nettie would fix it, but then we came down here and I don't know anything that's happening anymore."

Devlyn leaned forward. "Change is tough, but sudden changes are the worst. Jolie, if there's anything I can do to make your time here a little easier, just let me know." She gave Jolie one of her warm smiles. "Our town suffered an awful loss during the holidays. That fire came through and just stole our joy," she drawled softly. "But we aren't the kinds of folks that let stuff keep us down, so I am grateful to your daddy and his men for coming here and working to make things right. That's some good people right there."

Jolie stared at her. Then at Jess.

For a moment, Jess wondered if she was going to correct them, or say anything about Shane, but she didn't. She swallowed hard. Then she stood and motioned to a chair. "Can I read my book now?"

"Absolutely," Devlyn said, but while Jolie crossed to the comfortable big rocker-recliner, she aimed a look of question toward Jess.

Jess had no answer.

Jolie looked like her mother, but her quiet, brooding nature was nothing like the Chrissie they'd known. As she curled into the big chair, chin down, eyes on the thick book she'd brought along, it was like she'd deliberately tucked herself away. She'd lost her mother, her father had abandoned her and her brother, and she'd been dragged into a dank Tennessee winter. So maybe tucking herself away was a temporary defense.

Or maybe it was more.

That thought tweaked Jess's instincts.

Quietly absorbed in the story, Jolie stayed put, her iced tea forgotten, until Devlyn called the boys upstairs. And when she did, Jolie sighed, closed the book and stood. She didn't look around the cabin, noticing Mary's knack for mountain whimsy. The family of bears picnicking on a shelf, the line of bird nests her mother had found on nature walks, or the dried flowers tied in bouquets and hanging from above.

Sam had noticed right away.

But not his big sister, and Jess couldn't help but wonder why that was.

As they left, her mother's SUV rolled up the angled drive and Jess remained at the door to greet her. She owed her mother an apology. Coming back home had hot-wired some old triggers, but Jess wasn't a kid any longer. She was an educated adult and her mother and the people here in Kendrick Creek deserved nothing but respect.

Mary came through the door looking tired.

Really tired.

And that's when Jess realized she had stayed away too long. Her mother was no stranger to long days and nights, but the wise woman settling into a chair seemed drained. "Mom, are you all right?" Jess crossed the room and crouched by her mother's side. "You look done in."

Mary frowned in the direction of the clock. "I have been up since 5:45 a.m.," she reminded Jess.

True, but the diagnostician in Jess saw something else. Something deeper that made her pose the question and hate that she had to do it. "That's not it, is it?" Jess stayed where she was and held her mother's gaze. "I know you, Mom, and I know I haven't been back here in ages, but there's something going on. Please tell me what it is."

Mary didn't beat around the bush. She looked right into Jess's eyes and said a word that didn't just strike fear into Jess's heart. It seared that fear into her brain. "Glioblastoma."

Jess stared at her. She tried to form words, but nothing came out because they both understood the meaning behind that single-word diagnosis.

"Mom. No. Are you sure?" She choked the words out, hoping she'd misheard. Hoping her mother was wrong. But Mary Bristol was rarely wrong.

"I discovered it last year."

*Last year.*

Jess's eyes filled. Her throat clamped shut.

"I didn't want you worrying about me while you were going through your treatments," Mary explained gently, but then she'd always been gentle with Jess. Strong, yes. But gentle, too. Always putting Jess first. "I went to Texas for treatment, but it's come back. I was going to tell you over the Christmas break, but then the fire happened and you came down."

Tears filled Mary's eyes then slid down her cheeks. "I didn't mean to spring it on you with all of this, but you have to know now, Jess. Because there are things we have to do. To get ready."

Jess wanted to run. Wanted to hide. She longed to escape into the thick Appalachian forest and be alone for a while, to think. To process. To consider these words, but there was no time for any of that because she was an adult now. Only, at this moment, that was the last thing she wanted to be. "Oh, Mama."

Mary gathered her into a hug, a hug that felt both good and awful because Jess had missed years of hugs, and soon she was going to lose their comforting presence forever. She wanted to curse cancer. Condemn it. Cast it into the fire. But right now she had one job, to take care of the woman who had saved the life of a little girl and then kept right on saving it. "You wanted to spare me last year."

"You were fighting your own battle, and I wanted you to come out the other side, Jess. And you have."

Mary cradled Jess's tear-stained face with both hands. "Your prognosis has hope and that hope is something to cling to. I've had a good life, I have no regrets, and the good Lord blessed me when I answered the call to that car wreck forty-one years ago." She smiled through the tears, and the mix of feelings put a stranglehold on Jess's emotions. "He blessed me with you and now you're here to help me get things in order. The practice. My real estate. My people, Jess."

Her mother was so much more than a local doctor.

She was a sage. An optimist. A go-getter. A woman who never tired. She'd done so much in her seventy years. Jess's accomplishments paled in comparison. "Who knows about this?"

Mary shook her head. "Just me and Pastor Bob. Folks'll find out soon because the headaches are back. It could go like this for months," she added softly. "Or weeks."

Suddenly it felt like a cinder block sat on Jess's chest. She struggled to breathe. Why did this have to happen right now, right when she was feeling better? Stronger?

*Would you have preferred last year when you were in a fight for your life?*

Sacrificial love.

That was Mary Bristol's mantra, her mission. She'd never looked at life in the dollars and cents column. If she had, she'd have been charging higher rents on her buildings and higher fees for medical services.

Money had never been her goal.

Her mission had never been to simply save lives, but to help people, and that sparked a new clarity for Jess. "I'll do anything you need me to do, Mom. Anything."

"Just having you here is everything, honey." Mary leaned her forehead to Jess's, like she'd done for so many years. "I never expected your job to become a problem, or the fire to happen, but the chance to have my girl with me on this final walk is more than I could have hoped for. And more than I ever would have asked," she finished softly.

"Because you never ask help for yourself." Jess wrapped her arms around her mother again and just held her. "It's a lesson I've yet to learn."

"There's nothing wrong with chasing dreams," declared Mary in a firmer tone. "For now, I just want to get things as settled in town as I can before I'm too befuddled to make good decisions. And when that does happen," she said firmly, "I need you to make those decisions for me. Legally, everything is in order. Always has been, but that was simple enough with one child."

She smiled into Jess's eyes. "And now the fire damage allows me to leave this town with a new look, a pretty medical practice and maybe some greater hope, and that's something I realized when Shane Stone knocked on my door four days ago. A man with the know-how and the people to help. If that isn't a God thing, I don't know what is." She yawned, and Jess moved back.

"Can you make it upstairs all right?"

"Yes. But I think we'll have to switch rooms soon. Staying on the first floor would be the smart thing to do. I'd like to stay right here in my own house as long as possible, Jess." Mary stood up. She gazed around the log home with a winsome expression. "My memories are here. But if things get too bad, tuck me in a hospice home, all right?" She lifted those sweet blue eyes up to Jess. "No one ever knows how these things will go down in the end. But I've been happy living in this old place. I'll be fine going home to the Lord in it, too."

"I'll take care of it, Mom." Jess tried to make her voice strong and failed, but her mother simply smiled and patted her arm.

"I've had over a year to get used to this. Give it time, Jess. 'To everything there is a season.'" It was one of her mother's oft-quoted Bible verses.

Jess finished it for her. "And a time for every purpose under the heaven," she added softly.

"That's my girl." Mary turned. "My stomach's off." She sighed softly. "I'm going to pass on supper, okay?"

"Of course. You sure you don't want anything? Broth? Jell-O?"

Mary shook her head. "A good night's sleep is my current goal. G'night, honey." She went up the stairs.

Jess followed her with her eyes then sank onto the comfy plaid sofa her mother had bought years before.

The sofa smelled of the home she'd grown up in. A hint of cinnamon and vanilla, an old perfume her

# FREE BOOKS GIVEAWAY

2 FREE ROMANCE BOOKS!

2 FREE SUSPENSE BOOKS!

## GET UP TO FOUR FREE BOOKS & TWO FREE GIFTS WORTH OVER $20!

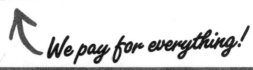

We pay for everything!

Dear Reader,

I am writing to announce the launch of a huge **FREE BOOK GIVEAWAY**... and to let you know that YOU are entitled to choose up to FOUR fantastic books that WE pay for.

Try **Love Inspired® Romance Larger-Print** books and fall in love with inspirational romances that take you on an uplifting journey of faith, forgiveness and hope.

Try **Love Inspired® Suspense Larger-Print** books where courage and optimism unite in stories of faith and love in the face of danger.

## Or TRY BOTH!

In return, we ask just one favor: Would you please participate in our brief Reader Survey? We'd love to hear from you.

This FREE BOOKS GIVEAWAY means that we pay for *everything!* We'll even cover the shipping, and no purchas is necessary, now or later. So please return your survey today. You'll get **Two Free Books** and **Two Mystery Gifts** from each series to try, altogether worth over **$20!**

Sincerely

*Pam Powers*

Pam Powers
For Harlequin Reader Servic

# Complete the survey below and return it today to receive up to 4 FREE BOOKS and FREE GIFTS guaranteed!

# FREE BOOKS GIVEAWAY
## Reader Survey

**1**

Do you prefer books which reflect Christian values?

○ YES    ○ NO

**2**

Do you share your favorite books with friends?

○ YES    ○ NO

**3**

Do you often choose to read instead of watching TV?

○ YES    ○ NO

**YES!** Please send me my Free Rewards, consisting of **2 Free Books from each series I select** and **Free Mystery Gifts**. I understand that I am under no obligation to buy anything, as explained on the back of this card.

❑ **Love Inspired® Romance Larger-Print** (122/322 IDL GQ36)
❑ **Love Inspired® Suspense Larger-Print** (107/307 IDL GQ36)
❑ **Try Both** (122/322 & 107/307 IDL GQ4J)

FIRST NAME                              LAST NAME

ADDRESS

APT #                CITY

STATE/PROV.          ZIP/POSTAL CODE

EMAIL ❑   Please check this box if you would like to receive newsletters and promotional emails from Harlequin Enterprises ULC and its affiliates. You can unsubscribe anytime.

LI/LIS-520-FBG21

mother loved. That vanilla-spiced scent was one of Jess's earliest memories.

She didn't remember being hospitalized or the long recovery. That had been blocked from her toddler memory, but the scent of someone caring about her was engraved in every fiber of her being.

Her mother's Bible sat on the table to her left.

She let her left hand trace the engraved letters embossed on the faux leather cover.

She slipped into the first-floor bedroom for a pillow and quilt, then came back down and curled up on the couch, breathing the scent of yesterday. She pretended it was so she would hear her mother if she needed help, but the truth was that she wanted to wrap herself in her mother's favorite scent as long as she could.

And that's exactly what she did.

Pouring rain put Monday's demolition on hold, but it didn't slow Shane. He hunkered down in the trailer, expanding his ideas digitally to use at the town meeting that night.

A sharp knock interrupted him shortly after Pete had headed over to the church. He got up and opened the door.

Miles Conrad stood on the other side. Mary had warned him that the central valley land owner wouldn't like Shane's ideas, but then Miles had never been a nice man. He owned the major community business not far from Kendall Mills Road. When the fire swept south, destroying numerous farms and homes, his Feed & Seed store emerged unscathed. Some folks would see the residential loss as a sorrow.

Miles was the type to see it as opportunity.

He didn't bother with pleasantries or small talk. He smacked an envelope into Shane's hand and almost got punched for his rudeness. Twenty years back, that might have been the outcome.

Fortunately, Shane had matured. Miles, however, had not. "What's this?"

"Cease and desist order. All new construction must stop," Miles demanded in the same patronizing tone Shane remembered from long ago. "The courts want to review the permissions the town has given you."

At Miles's behest, no doubt, but this wasn't Shane's first rodeo. "This is an unincorporated town, Miles."

Miles scowled. "The law's the law."

"The law is actually on my side," Shane told him in an easy voice, his calm heightening the other man's discomfiture. "I'm not building new. I'm replacing. And as long as the buildings meet or exceed code, I'm legal. Worse, you know that and were hoping I didn't," he went on. "I'm not sure what that says about this situation, but if you'll excuse me, I have work to do." He reached forward to shut the trailer door, but Miles blocked it with his hand.

"You're nothing to this town, Stone."

Funny how the words hurt, even after all this time.

"You came from nothing and you're still nothing but an ex-con, always looking to take what's not his. Hiding behind a hard hat and a bunch of trucks doesn't change you. Just dresses you up a little."

Shane pulled the door shut.

He didn't want to. Part of him wanted to go toe-to-toe with the obnoxious landowner and have his say, but the best defense against a man like Conrad was to ignore him.

He wouldn't like being ignored, and if he thought prettying up the town messed up his chances at getting a highway spur through his land, that was his problem. Not Shane's. And having people hate you for something you didn't do was a price he'd paid long ago. Yeah, it was rough, but in the end, totally worth it.

He finished his layout for the presentation and was just heading out the door when a big truck rolled into the small parking lot where they'd parked the work trailer. A big, burly man swung down from the driver's seat.

Bobby Ray Carlson.

He hadn't seen Bobby Ray in years, and the football player hadn't lost any height and had stayed trim. And he was still huge. "Bobby Ray." Shane moved forward, unsure what was about to transpire. "How are you?"

Bobby Ray extended his hand and his grip was every bit as strong as the man behind it. "I'm all right, Shane, but my town's seen trouble while I was gone." He was wearing a rugged camo cap. He reached and moved it back slightly. The rain had tapered to a sprinkle. Bobby Ray didn't seem to notice. "I was at my in-laws' place for the holidays when stuff fell apart around here. I got back yesterday in time for the kids to go back to school and heard what you were doing. Man, Shane." He folded his arms across his broad chest and whistled. "You've got guts."

"For coming back?"

"No, sir, for having what it takes to come back and take charge," Bobby Ray declared. "I know Miles Conrad is going to be fuming, but when I came through town and saw the damage and the demo, I thought, *I want to be part of this*. Because it's epic," he told Shane. "My great-granddaddy helped build things here, and he wouldn't have kowtowed to the Conrads then and I don't aim to do it now. I've got dumps and excavators and big shovels. Let me get your demo out of the way for you, clear your sites, and you'll have clear sailing."

Demo cleanup and disposal?

That would be a huge contribution to the effort. And after Miles's visit, Shane could hardly believe it. "Bobby Ray, I—"

"Many hands make light work," Bobby Ray added cheerfully. "My mama had that saying engraved on my forehead while I was growing up, and it's as true now as it was then. If you pull things apart and put 'em back together, me and my three guys will take care of the in-between."

"That saves us a lot of rental fees."

"And helps the town, so we're good to go." He reached out a hand and when he met Shane's gaze, Shane read the sincerity in the big man's eyes. "It's good to have you back, Shane. Real good. And there's a bunch of us feelin' that way. Just so you know."

He knew, too.

Bobby Ray didn't have to say anything, but Shane read it in the thrust of his chin, the firmness of his expression, as if he was saying more than words. Because he was.

How many others knew the truth? Shane wondered as he shook the man's hand.

"I'll see you up the road," Bobby Ray said as he turned and climbed back into his big rig.

A mix of emotions swamped Shane as he watched the truck rumble through town.

Maybe he shouldn't have brought the kids here. Maybe he should have let them stay back in Maryland, but three months had seemed like forever.

Could he keep the truth about what he'd done for his sister from Sam and Jolie?

He had to. But Devlyn was right. People talked.

Now he just had to make sure they didn't talk about it around his precious children.

## Chapter Eleven

Jess walked into the town hall a few minutes after six that evening. Jenny Billings had stayed at the clinic with Hassie, and Jess had insisted that Mary stay at home and rest.

Mary had ignored the suggestion. "I intend to do things while I still can," she'd told Jess once they'd gotten into the SUV. "Don't put me out to pasture too early, Jess. I don't do well left to my own devices."

"It's hard," Jess had admitted with a mock frown. "I'm supposed to treat you like it's all normal while you're fighting brain cancer? I'm not an actress, Mom."

"Every doctor has that in them," Mary had replied practically. "Knowing who can handle the whole truth and who wants things veiled. Not everyone wants their prognosis laid out in spades. And if my stomach behaves itself, we'll do all right tonight."

Her mother was right, but it had only been twenty-two hours since she'd told Jess the truth. Obviously that was all the time she was going to get. "How was Hassie this afternoon?"

Mary frowned. "I think she's got permanent lung damage and she won't go to the hospital."

"Why not?"

"She says everyone she's ever taken there has left the world, and if she's going to leave, it will be on her own ground."

Well, that sounded familiar since her mother fairly echoed those wishes the night before. But there was one major difference. "What about their great-grand-daughters?"

Mary winced as Jess pulled into the parking area adjacent to the high school. "Ed can't handle them on his own. They can barely handle it together, and if the county looks into things, we'll have a problem. Ed and Hassie aren't the type to hand family over easily, so it's a bind. We pray. We counsel. We move on," she told Jess.

Practical. Straightforward. Focused.

Her mother was all of these things, but the thought of spinning that many plates boggled Jess. She was accustomed to having a plan. Even in the chronically busy E.R., there was always a plan.

The life of a country doctor was quite different.

A couple of men were smoking outside. They raised their hands to Mary. "Good to see you, Doc."

"Sorry about your place, Doc," said the second man. "I'm making a table for your new setup," he added. "And I picked up the old one to refinish. There's life in it yet."

"Thank you, Willis."

"My pleasure, Doc."

Jess spoke softly as they approached the door. "I don't know how to do this." She swept the damaged town a look of consideration. "People and places and tables, kids in rough situations, weighing the odds and knowing who to call an ambulance for and who to let fade away. We're making life-and-death decisions we have no right to make, Mom."

"We're letting them make the decisions, honey."

That was another minor shock wave.

"You've been part of a big team effort in New York." Mary drew Jess to one side as a middle-aged couple approached. "There's a practiced method for every situation, correct?"

"Because we have hundreds of people seeking care every day," Jess replied. "It might look confusing to others, but it's organized chaos because everyone knows their job and does it. Like a well-oiled machine."

"It's different here," Mary admitted. "Each person, each situation, each family, is unique. Down here, I work on saving lives week to week. Month to month. Year to year. I know my patients. And they know me. And so it's different."

She knew her patients.

Her words humbled Jess. She'd been in Manhattan for over fifteen years and could honestly say she only knew a handful of people. She saw tons of patients, ran a tight ship, and worked with dozens of folks, but she could count only a handful of people she knew personally. Some of her friends had married and moved on.

Some had left the city to work elsewhere. Now, it was a smattering of friends she rarely saw, because no one had time to see anyone.

"Ladies, I saved seats for you two."

Shane's voice interrupted her thoughts as he came their way from inside the school hall. She shifted her attention to him. "That's real nice, Shane. Thank you."

"Pure selfishness, ma'am." He smiled down at Jess and she found herself smiling back as if they were old friends when they were anything but. That didn't change the warmth of his smile or the effect on her pulse. "I want to keep people who might support my ideas close at hand in case they don't go over well."

"I expect Miles paid you a visit." Mary sent the brash property owner a sideways glance but kept her attention on Shane. "He tried to get my attention at the clinic, but we were busy with patients and I sent him on his way."

"He came by. I called him out. He went away. I was pretty sure he'd be here, but he doesn't have a leg to stand on for the rebuilds, and that's going to scorch him."

"Nothing new about that," Mary noted and then walked forward, head high, taking a seat right up front, next to Shane's computer bag.

"I need to learn that trick," Jess said.

Shane tipped his gaze back to hers. "What trick?"

"Keeping my cool. She gives and gives, and never loses her way. I thought my life was frenzied in the ER, but it's mostly ordered and ridiculously efficient."

"I sense a 'but' coming." He stepped aside to let her

precede him as they moved left to access the front of
the filling room.

"But I don't know a soul," she told him. "I don't
know my patients, or their families, or what's going on
in their lives. They're just a scrawl on a whiteboard or
letters on a computer screen, and then they're gone."

"Normal for the city, isn't it?" he asked as they got
to the front of the auditorium.

Five board members took seats on the old stage, three
men and two women. Flora Buckner had done her hair
for the meeting while Jordan Ash's long, blond pony-
tail was pulled up in a messy knot on top of her head,
looking a lot like it had looked a quarter-century ago.

She spotted Jess, grinned and waved, then took her
seat as the meeting was called to order.

Jess sat beside her mother, surrounded by people
who'd just gone through a disaster. Yet the room wasn't
anxiety-filled; it teemed with hope.

When Shane gave his short presentation of how he
saw the new and renovated buildings on their short
Main Street, the majority didn't scorn a former thief.

They welcomed his help and expertise in something
so close to a benediction she didn't know what else to
call it.

Then Miles Conrad stalked to the podium.

His stance, his presence and the coldness of his expression cast a chill. He swept the room a long look before raising a sheaf of papers in his hand. "We've stood
together in tough times before." He raised the papers
higher. "We gathered right here nearly twenty-eight
years ago after a storm turned the creek into a raging

river that created a disaster for a lot of good, hardworking folks. And when we set up a plan to raise money to fix things, to make things better for those who suffered most, a local boy tried to steal thousands of dollars that *you* raised."

He paused to make eye contact with as many people as possible. "Your good will raised those funds. And then Shane Stone tried to steal them. Bold as brass, that *boy*, sitting right there—" he pointed to Shane "—tried to turn your efforts into nothing. Why, if it wasn't for Mary's girl, finding him red-handed, he might've gotten away with it. But he didn't." Miles gripped the podium with both hands, like a revival preacher, while Jess's heart hammered in her chest, wishing—

Wishing he hadn't done it. But he had, and Miles wasn't about to let bygones be bygones.

A ripple of unease passed through the crowd, but when Miles held up a paper, a mugshot of Shane taken at age eighteen, murmurs increased.

"We're not a big town," Miles reminded them. "This is a small town, with small-town values, and we stand with one another when things get rough. There's no way we should be embracing help from someone who tried to steal from us once, because the old sayin' holds true. Fool me once, shame on you. Fool me twice…" He paused and let his gaze wander the room. "Shame on me. And I'm here to say that if we let the likes of Shane Stone try to mess with us again, then the fault isn't on him." Miles shook his head and had the nerve to look aggrieved. "It's on you and me. And that's all I've got to say."

When the central valley landowner walked back to his seat, Jess expected Shane to stand and refute his words.

He didn't.

He sat right there, letting Conrad's words sink in and maybe take root, as if a person couldn't grow and change and—

"Shame on you, Miles." A strong male voice rang out from the back of the room. Jess turned.

So did Shane and her mother as Bobby Ray moved forward. "I am not registered to speak tonight," Bobby Ray told the council, "but my mama would take a switch to me if I let something like this go past and not raise a ruckus. This ain't about what's gone on nearly thirty years back." He braced his hands on his hips when he got to the front of the room and faced the council, then the crowd. "This is about good people reaching out. In these past three decades, when has Miles ever reached into his back pocket to offer a hand out or a hand up?"

Bobby Ray knew enough to pause and let his words sink in.

"But when Shane Stone heard about our troubles, he didn't just jump in his truck and head south with two little kids he uprooted. He brought a pack of trucks and know-how. My mama always taught me how actions speak louder than words, and I think we have a prime example of that right here in Kendrick Creek this week.

"Now while some folks have turned their Christmas lights off because the holiday season just ended, I say we drag them lights back out, and light up this town with hope while Shane and his crew are here. Welcome them the way a town like ours should. Because there are givers and there are takers in this world, and no matter what went on in a boy's head twenty-seven years ago, the man that's here tonight is a giver. And me and my boys, we're going to be working alongside him. And that's all I've got to say." He nodded to the council, then crossed the room to shake Shane's hand. When he did, he clapped Shane on the back. "It's good to have you back, Shane."

Shane looked at Bobby Ray directly. "Good to be here."

Miles stood again.

The council ignored him.

Instead they thanked Shane for his ideas, offered quick approval, then adjourned the meeting to let everyone enjoy the Kendrick Creek Ladies' Fellowship's punch and cookies at tables set up along the far wall.

People surrounded Shane. He spoke to everyone, taking notes on one of the smallest scratchpads Jess had ever seen.

"I'd like to stay and mingle for a few minutes, Jess." Mary stood slowly, staying in place for a few seconds to gain her equilibrium. "Not long, though."

It wasn't the red punch and cookies that drew her mother to the gathering area. It was the people, and Jess walked alongside her as she moved forward. As folks greeted Mary with a mix of smiles and commiseration over the damage her properties had suffered, the real affection was apparent.

*I know mine and mine know me.*

Emotion rose within Jess as the old words from John's Gospel came back. She'd forgotten what it was like to be known. Even being on extended sick leave for almost a year of cancer treatments, there were few people in the city who'd looked in on her. Except for her mother's steady calls and a few medical buddies, that was it.

She watched people gather around her mother in an outpouring of affection and gratitude, and for the first time in a long time, she recognized the wealth in Mary's life. Wealth that had nothing to do with worldly goods and everything to do with gifts of the heart.

"We all love your mom."

Jess turned to see that Jordan had come up alongside her. "I haven't seen you since I left for med school, Jordan. How are you? How is everything? You look wonderful, and I'm pretty sure that you're the only person from our graduating class who hasn't changed because I'd recognize you anywhere."

Jordan hugged her.

Though Jess often claimed she wasn't a hugger, it felt good to hug her old friend.

"I am caught in a storm of what-ifs. And who knows how that's going to come out?" Jordan told her once she'd stepped back. Then she noted Jess's chemo hat with a sympathetic grimace. "Who'd have thought things would be this way when we sat in that gymnasium on graduation day?"

"Not me," Jess said honestly. "I had my life all planned out."

"Always did." Jordan commended her. "From the time you were a little kid, you planned your work and worked your plan. No one was surprised to see you become a big-city doctor, Jess. But I'm real sorry about the cancer."

"You sent me a card last year."

"Well, you were up there all alone. I didn't even know if you'd remember me," she admitted.

Jess hadn't thought to send notes back, to thank people for their good wishes. Now she realized she should have done that. "How could I forget one of my best friends in school? The Four Musketeers, remember?"

"How could I possibly forget?" Jordan laughed, then squeezed Jess's arm. "You, me, Devlyn and Amy Sue. We had so many plans, didn't we? Chock-full of dreams and goals. Good things," she added with a wistful note.

"So what happened with yours?" asked Jess, and Jordan frowned.

"Engaged twice, broke it off both times, ran the Dollar Friendly until the fire took it, and saved money to open my own general store," Jordan told her. "So now—a crossroads."

"I don't even know what a general store is," Jess confessed.

"Think eclectic and cool, a mix of old-fashioned items, pure South and fun new ideas. My goal was to rent one of your mama's buildings, the old hardware store. It's in plain sight of the Foothills Parkway. A plan like Shane's could help draw some of that tourist money in, and that would be a blessing."

"I couldn't believe how things have grown," Jess replied. "Pigeon Forge. Sevierville. And Devlyn said it's the same in Gatlinburg. Can a little town like this do enough business, Jordy?" The old nickname seemed just as natural today as it had twenty years ago.

"I think it can," Jordan replied. "There are a bunch

of cabin rentals here now. And if folks get off the parkway at Wilton Springs, a cozy ride through small-town America brings them to our doorstep, but we need to have a reason to make them stop to check things out. That beautiful apple orchard draws its share, but then folks motor on through.

"The cabin rentals will help," she pointed out. "A lot of folks like the peace of the mountains even though they want to visit the attractions. I think we've got a solid shot." Jordy indicated Shane with her eyes. "If Shane's right, maybe this fire will be a blessing in disguise for some. And then those can help others. Having him and you back to help makes it seem like there's a power shift going on, and that's what we need to have things happen. Between your mother, Shane, and now Bobby Ray, we could see real change here. And I'm glad you came back to help your mom." Jordan laid a hand on Jess's arm. "It's good to have you here, Jess."

Jordan's sincerity only increased Jess's guilt. "It's good to be back. But it's weird, Jordy, and I can't pretend it's not."

"Then give it time to get *un*weird," Jordan told her as they moved toward Mary.

"I'm ready for twenty minutes of reading and a good night's sleep," announced Mary when they approached.

Mary said she wanted normal, so Jess answered in kind, though she could clearly see the weariness in her mother's expression. "Sounds good." She smiled at her mother then lifted her gaze to Shane. There it was again. That connection.

As if something new and maybe even beautiful happened whenever their eyes met. When that lower muscle in his cheek flexed slightly.

Mary tucked her arm through Jess's and she understood the unspoken message. Mary needed to get home. "I could use a solid night's sleep myself," Jess agreed.

"Shane, we'll see you tomorrow, all right?"

"First thing," he promised. "Thanks for being here tonight. Both of you."

"Glad to do it," said Jess as she guided Mary to the door. "Jordy, so nice to see you."

"You, too, Jess. Mary, are you all right?" Jordy might not have a medical background, but she'd known Jess's mother since the girls had started playing together nearly forty years ago.

"Tired, Jordy. And maybe a touch of that stomach bug rolling around."

Jordy put her hands out, palms facing Mary and Jess. "I'm backing off so I don't catch it. See you both soon."

"Will do," Jess replied. No stranger to the indignities of cancer, she asked her mother in a softer tone, "Are you going to be sick?"

"Yes."

When Mary was more in control a few minutes later, Jess tucked her into the SUV and drove up the road.

It had felt odd to pull into the driveway last week, but now the mountain house seemed to welcome Jess, which made this whole thing feel more like home than anything she'd known in a long time.

But how was it going to feel once her beloved mother was gone?

* * *

Pete met Shane at the door of the cabin. He'd taken charge of the kids so that Shane could make his presentation to the town. "Went well, I take it?"

"It did."

"Good."

Pete shrugged into his jacket. "Kids are asleep. Dishes done. I'll see you in the morning."

"Thanks, Pete."

Shane tossed his jacket onto a wall hook and drew a deep breath. When he'd brought his crew down to offer assistance to a town that believed he'd betrayed them, he couldn't have anticipated the pull on his heart the moment he spotted Jess in that car.

They were both here to help, and that put them on the same side at long last. And when she'd cheered his proposal, when he'd met her gaze from the podium, he hadn't wanted to break the connection.

The internal warning bell sounded more like a gong right now. Jess was amazing, but she put more faith in the teachings of man than God. He embraced the thought that the two worked hand in hand. He had to keep the truth from the kids, which would be tougher than he'd thought given the people who knew what actually happened. And, to top it off, he didn't dare put the kids in cancer's crosshairs again.

But as he set the coffee maker to switch on automatically in the morning, something else stirred him.

Change.

Shane didn't like change. He preferred to know what was happening in two weeks, six months, the coming year. He scheduled jobs inside of jobs to layer the most effective work production he could maneuver and kept his finger on the pulse of every project. Here it was different because old ties tugged him in multiple directions.

His phone buzzed a text. He lifted the phone and saw Jess's words. Great job tonight.

He wanted to text her back. Have one of those silly text conversations that moved things forward between them.

He didn't do that. He sent a simple thumbs-up emoji instead.

He didn't have the option to explore the unexpected with Jess, but seeing her, talking to her, made him want to.

He couldn't.

He wasn't in Kendrick Creek to complicate his life. It was knotted enough.

But he wasn't blind to the feelings swirling inside him, a hole that narrowed when Jess was around.

He went out onto the broad front porch. Graham had rebuilt the supports and added country-style railings. A pair of matching rocking chairs flanked a small table next to a stack of seasoned firewood. Above the unforested section of yard, a generous pattern of stars shone in the dark night sky.

The beauty of this land called to him. The rolling waves of the Blue Ridge were steeped in his bones. He'd worked so hard to show the world that he wasn't the person he'd pretended to be to save Chrissie. He'd stayed the course so that his goodness and honesty became his stake in the growing business, but being here didn't seem to be the answer he sought. It just seemed to bring more questions.

*Be still...*

The old words had been a huge comfort to him in prison.

*Be still and know that I am God.*

He took another deep breath, and the peace of the moment softened the questioning edges.

He didn't have all the answers. God did. He tended to get into trouble when he forgot that. He needed to keep his faith front and center. With the mostly gentle hearts of the town, that shouldn't be a problem, except for one heart in particular and that one, well—

That one had been problematic for a very long time.

## Chapter Twelve

"I hate needing help. And having people know I'm not well." Mary gripped Jess's sleeve as they went up the two steps to the front porch.

"You like to project an image of strength," noted Jess. "So do I," she admitted as she reached to unlock her mother's front door. "But one thing I've learned is that sometimes it's better to face it head-on instead of letting folks wonder. Because you know that's what they'll do," she finished. From a couple of looks cast their way tonight, Jess was pretty sure some people were already wondering. "So why not be upfront about it?"

A single tear trickled down Mary's cheek as they slowly moved inside. It broke Jess's heart to see it, but still she waited, the question hanging between them.

"To have folks knowing means I have to deal with folks knowing."

"They'll want a chance to say goodbye, Mom. And you could have months left, but if you don't—"

"Stupid cancer." Disgust thickened Mary's voice.

"I know."

Mary sighed then gripped Jess's hand. "We've done all right for ourselves, haven't we? The Bristol women have left their mark on this world."

"And helped a lot of people," Jess reminded her. "Maybe it's their turn to help you, Mom. Even though your stubborn, independent spirit doesn't take well to that."

A tiny smile of admission softened her mother's jaw. "All right." She shrugged out of her coat and handed it to Jess. "I haven't shrunk from anything all my life, and I don't want to start now. Me and the Lord and a cast of friends. We've got this."

Her mother hated attention, but she was right. The time had come to be forthright, with the town moving forward. And what did that mean for her mother's properties?

Dissolution? Selling?

Jess couldn't think of that. Right now she wanted to keep her mother calm and comfortable while Jess would wage her own private spiritual war.

"Mom, how about if you take the downstairs bedroom tonight and I'll sleep upstairs?" Jess asked. "No sense going up and down those stairs if your stomach's reeling."

"The couch is closer." Mary didn't even attempt to get into pajamas. She sank onto the couch, curled up and was asleep within two minutes. Was it the cancer waging war with her gut? Or the nasty virus that several patients had recently reported?

Jess didn't know.

She turned off the lights and let the silence wrap itself around her. It didn't feel as odd tonight. The beautiful, rustic home held so many good memories, but the most important part of the setting wouldn't be here much longer. Jess hated that, and she hated that she had no one to talk to. She pulled out her phone and sent Shane a text, complimenting him on how he handled the meeting. She waited, hoping it would open a conversation.

It didn't. He sent back a thumbs-up emoji. That was it.

She stared at the phone, knowing he was right to keep his distance. Chrissie's kids didn't need confusion in their lives, and cancer liked to leave a cloud of confusion in its wake. So be it.

Jess climbed the stairs. She thought she'd never fall asleep, but something about crawling into her mother's bed, feeling the presence of such a strong woman throughout this house, was like being held in a blanket of love. A blanket that gave her nearly seven full hours of sleep that wasn't just welcome. It was absolutely needed.

Shane did an early lumber pickup on Route 321 for some special cuts that hadn't been available the previous day. He almost passed by the Celtic bakery that had opened back when he was a teen, but he turned in at the last minute. The kids would love the small pound cakes and he had a penchant for their cinnamon-raisin-filled pastry things. But it was the fudge tarts that made him pull into the parking area and hop out of the truck.

Jess used to love those fudge tarts.

He refused to think about that, or to ponder his welcome in the store. If he second-guessed every stop he made in Kendrick Creek, nothing would get done. There wasn't time to mess around, anyway. His pastry order had been packed quickly, and with full-on Southern charm, and he was back on the road a few minutes later.

He was supposed to meet Jess and Mary at the clinic to go over the final plans for the medical office, but when he got there, Jess was the only one inside. He noted the half-closed office door that indicated Hassie was resting and motioned that way. "Is Mary in back with Hassie?"

"She's home."

It wasn't the words that spiked his concern. Or that it was unusual for a woman like Doc Bristol to miss an important meeting, because she'd always been a force to be reckoned with.

It was remembering the slack in Mary's features the night before and the unusual weariness that deepened the shadows beneath her eyes.

Her absence this morning stirred more doubt. He perched one hip on the corner of the desk and decided to level the playing field. "What's going on, Jess?" he posed the question gently, and her one-word reply made him want to kick something.

"Cancer."

His heart ached, but that explained Mary's urgency to get things done fast.

"When it rains, it appears to pour," she whispered, and he wasn't sure if she was whispering so that Hassie wouldn't hear or because she couldn't find her voice to talk out loud. "She discovered it last year and had treatment, but it was only a stopgap. And she never told me because I was going through treatment, so she handled it all herself. It's in her brain, Shane. She's become symptomatic again, and all my pricey medical training and experience can't help the one person who needs me most. My mother."

He remembered when she was young, how her hands would shake with anger when people did stupid things. Her hands shook now. Not with grief, but anger at her inability to make this better. He reached out and grasped her hands to make the shaking stop. "I'm sorry, Jess. So sorry."

"I hate this." Her voice held despair. "I hate it so much, that she went through that treatment in Texas all alone because she wanted to protect me while I was fighting my own fight. It's always been that way, Shane."

She lifted her eyes to his, and the sorrow that filled them was more than tears. It was pure anguish. "She sacrificed for me from the time she found me on the roadside and she never stopped. It didn't matter where I was, I always knew she was here. That home was here. And now it won't be because she'll be gone and I'm pretty sure my stupid heart is breaking apart right now even though I'm trying to be brave."

"Jess." He didn't mean to hug her, but he couldn't stop himself. He gathered her into his arms and just held on. "She doesn't need you to be brave as much as she just needs you," he said softly. "To be with her. To let her cry or talk, and you do the same. It's not about courage, Jess, you've got your share of that," he went on while trying to ignore how good and right it felt to hold her. Support her. How perfect it was to feel her cheek pressed against his chest. "It's about being here. Having you here will be the best medicine for her, but I can't say how sorry I am, because your mother was one of the few people who saw good in me from the get-go. She sent at least one card or letter to me every month I was in prison, and she talked about hope and the future. The letters I got from some people here gave me the strength to hang on. To find faith. And to move forward in my life. You can't know how much that meant to me," he finished.

She hiccupped, or sobbed softly, he wasn't sure which, but as he held her, her body relaxed against his. She lifted her head and sighed. "How'd you get so smart, Shane?"

"I follow the best carpenter known to man," he told her honestly. When she raised an eyebrow, he explained. "Building teaches you things," he told her. "How to square things up, balance a load, to use the best quality materials you can find, and to always have a good level in the toolbox, because a tilted house can't ever stand straight. And those are life lessons you can take to the bank."

She dropped her forehead to his chest for a few seconds then eased back. Looked up. Met his gaze.

He wanted to kiss her.

Weren't things already messed up enough for them? But the urge to see what it would be like to kiss Jess

Bristol spurred him to cradle her face in his hands. Gaze into those honey-toned eyes. See the longing there, the same emotion currently driving him. But even as she tipped her head slightly to test the waters, he pulled back.

Not because he wanted to. Because he *had* to.

She was vulnerable now. Taking advantage of that would be a crummy thing to do. So maybe he was a jerk for wanting it so badly when her world was crumbling around her.

She ducked away, snatched a handful of tissues and stepped back. "No one else knows about this, Shane."

"Mary's been a mainstay in this town a long time," he told her. "If she's been off her game at all, folks have noticed and probably been too polite to say anything because they love her."

His words hit home. She accepted his statement with a look of resignation. "You're right, of course. It's always better to handle things as if they're normal, even if it's a new normal that no one wants. Have you got the layout for the office renovation? Mom asked me to glance at the plans, give you a thumbs-up and send you on your way so we don't delay any longer."

"Now that sounds like Mary." He unrolled his sketch and Jess whistled lightly.

"That's a beautiful setup, Shane." She leaned over the page, smelling like a combination of rich vanilla and something warm and spiced. It reminded him of autumn afternoons and something else…something earthy and raw. Totally Jess.

She glanced up at him to pose a question and caught

him inhaling. She gave him a sharp elbow jab to the gut then tapped an unpolished nail to the rendering below. "Pay attention."

"Oh, I was." He smiled at her, hoping she'd smile back, and when she did it felt like a NASCAR victory lap, even though they both knew better.

She stayed focused, but he'd noticed the spark in her eye before she'd returned her attention to the office layout. "I'd suggest we increase the size of this bathroom for people with mobility challenges, and this stock closet."

She pointed to another section. "And the skylight here is nice, but they leak sometimes, don't they?"

"If not properly maintained, they could."

"Then let's ditch that, although I know we have some long dark days in December and January."

"How about dormer windows to let in diffused light?" he suggested.

When she nodded, he penciled them into the drawings.

"Except that will cost extra, won't it? You know how Mom is about spending money we don't have to spend."

"She did give you approval rights, Jess." When she looked over her shoulder at him, he put a hand on her back and met her gaze again. "She did that because she trusts you. Go with your gut. It's served you well over the years. I'm pretty sure the same thing will happen now."

Would it?

Right now Jess's gut was telling her one thing and her head was saying something quite different. The hand resting on her back offered a comfort she didn't dare seek.

Shane didn't just draw her, which was odd enough considering their past.

The attraction to him tugged her, urging her to find out more because Shane was different than anyone else she'd known. Even with so many things swirling around her, this man was a cornerstone. A living force of kindness and goodness and strength. In all her forty-three years, she'd never reacted to a man like this before, and it had been…what? A week?

Ridiculous.

She'd had relationships before. Who hadn't?

But this?

The scent of him, leather and smooth erasers and plain old soap invited her to step closer when they both knew that was impossible. When he stepped back, she was able to draw a breath—a deep one—for the first time since he'd tugged her into an embrace long minutes before.

But their lives were quite different. She'd only be in Kendrick Creek as long as Mary was here, most likely. And then she'd move on to whatever job offer tempted her the most.

Shane would head back to Maryland, building new neighborhoods or fixing up old ones, giving people their life-long dream of a home.

Shane tapped the plans with his free hand. "I'm jumping on this once Bobby Ray has cleared the debris. I don't know what your mom's timeline is, but I want her to see it done, and if God gives her time to reopen her practice in the new digs…well, good. If not, I want her to see what her love and devotion have brought to this town. What's her prognosis, Jess?"

"Short, most likely," she said softly. Then she squared her shoulders. "But we'll take whatever time we get and you know she'll bug you to get the building next door done quickly so Devlyn can set up there. Mom's worried about her."

"No insurance and a total loss is reason to be worried," he acknowledged. "Devlyn took a major hit just when her business was starting to take off. That's a tough one."

Funny how she wouldn't have considered a house-front startup as a money-making enterprise a few weeks ago, but she saw the value now. Another lesson learned. "Hassie Trembeth wants to go home today," she told him.

"Is she improving?" Shane posed the question then grimaced when Jess shook her head.

"No, but she's not worse, either. She's stable enough to be home with oxygen, but certainly not capable of caring for little kids."

"How'd she take that?" He kept his voice low with a glance toward the back room.

"Resigned. She knows her lungs are deteriorating, and she doesn't want to spend her last days in a hospital, but she isn't ready to ask for hospice. Stubborn."

Shane disagreed. "Cautious," he told her. "If she requests hospice, wouldn't the caregivers be required to report that she can't take care of the girls? And that goes straight to a social worker, then the county, and she loses what she fought for. The chance to make sure her great-granddaughters get off to a good start."

A good start.

Like the one she'd gotten with Mary.

Just then, a large flatbed rolled up the road and Shane moved to the door. "Time to go."

"Shane." She moved forward when he turned to leave and put her hands out. He gripped them with his. "Thank you."

"Just doin' my job, ma'am." He smiled at her, a more self-assured smile than the one she remembered as a sixteen-year-old. "Keep me posted."

"Will do."

He jogged across the street to meet the delivery driver and several of his construction crew. She watched, wondering if he'd glance back.

He didn't, although she wanted him to, but right now they needed to focus on moving forward, and there was no time to waste.

The thought of Mary's prognosis spurred Shane on.

He didn't pull workers off other jobs. Those were important, too, but when he laid out the schedule for the men assigned to the medical office crew, they looked surprised by the extended hours. Then one of the guys pointed to the demolished south side of Mary's offices. "Piece of cake, boss. It's not like I need to be home at six o'clock down here. If you need extra time, you've got it."

When the other men agreed, Shane knew they were on the right track.

He noticed several patients going in and out of the

makeshift clinic as he worked on rebuilding the outer walls, and when he saw Ed guiding Hassie to their car, he hurried over to help. "Heading home, Miss Hassie?"

"I am, son." She met his gaze forthright. Her shortness of breath and the graveled sound of her voice made the lung damage clear. "I am blessed by the good care I've gotten, and to have a home to go to, but a woman doesn't leave things undone, and I've got some figuring to do. Important stuff."

Ed guided her arm as Shane opened the passenger-side door. "We'll figure it all out, Mother. Sophie's got the girls now, and they couldn't be in better hands."

"Except Sophie's only a couple years younger than we are." Hassie had to catch her breath between the words.

"I know." The old man eased her into the car with Shane's help, then leaned in slightly. "I'll make sure things are done your way, Mother. Those girls have me on their side. I promise."

Hassie's old eyes watered. The look she gave him, a look of love tempered with reality, knifed Shane's heart. "I know you will, Ed. I know you will."

Shane understood what she couldn't say.

Ed was a good man. He tried hard. But it was Hassie who'd kept their plates spinning. If Ed was the muscle, Hassie was the brains of their operation. Without her, the weakened old man would never be able to care for the girls. Would he be strong enough to stand his ground and make decisions about their care when Hassie was gone?

Hassie put her hand over her husband's and smiled.

"God will provide, Ed. He always does. He put those girlies in our lives when everything crumbled around them. He won't abandon them now."

"He never does, Mother." Ed smiled at her.

She smiled back. Then Ed rounded the car as Shane shut the door.

Hassie looked up at Shane through the open window with an expression of such love and compassion that he knew instantly she was in on his secret. The old woman didn't have to say a word. It was there in her expression. The warmth of her eyes. "I'll check in, Miss Hassie." He slipped her a small package of butter rum candies and her appreciation made him feel like it was so much more than a dollar pack of candy.

"You do that and take care of those children the Lord put in your path," she replied. "Mary told me what happened, and while it's a sorrowful thing, how good for those kids to have you, Shane. The Lord giveth, and the Lord taketh away. And when He made you, He made a giver. From the get-go."

Yep. She knew.

But she went no further, and as he returned to his crew, he didn't dare take time to wonder who else was aware of what he'd done. How could he protect the kids from hearing loose talk, especially now that they were in school?

*You can't.*

The reality of the simple words cut him because he'd sacrificed a lot for this secret.

*What if it's not up to you any longer?*

The thought humbled Shane. He was accustomed to

being in charge. It became ingrained once he was running his own business with Pete.

After being locked up and under someone else's control, he knew he never wanted to deal with a situation like that again. So was he man enough to cede control to God? To live the words he spoke in prayer?

He wasn't sure, and while he hoped he wouldn't have to find out, a new thought came to him.

He'd dealt with a lot throughout his life and he'd not only survived, he'd thrived. And despite what Jolie and Sam might hear while they were in Kendrick Creek, they would, too. Because they had him and the gift of faith.

Together, they could move mountains.

## Chapter Thirteen

"**W**here's Mary?" Miles Conrad burst through the door of the temporary medical office a little after four that afternoon. He leveled Jess a stern look as if she were a child. "I need to talk to her, sooner rather than later."

Jess had finished with the last patients of the day, she'd changed the sheets on Hassie's bed, sanitized the room, and set out fresh gowns in case they had an overnight emergency. She'd turned down the heat and was just about to head home when Miles barged in.

His crossed-arm stance set her on edge, but she'd faced a lot of grumpy people in the ER. She summoned up a calm she didn't feel and faced him directly. "Good afternoon, Miles. Are you feeling poorly? Do you need to see a doctor?"

Her pretense of caring deepened his scowl. "You might not be blood, but the apple sure didn't fall far from the Bristol tree when Mary dragged you out of the forest. You were a smart aleck growing up. And the same now. I'm not here to seek medical attention. As if." He scoffed to let her know what he thought of that option. "Where's your mother?"

She had to take a deep breath to tamp down her reaction, and it worked, but only because she'd had years of practice. "Mom's tending other things. I've got today's shift here." She kept her tone level, mostly to agitate him because he liked getting folks riled up. It had always disappointed him when his antics drew no reaction.

"At home?"

"The day's over, Miles."

"Mr. Conrad to you."

"All right." She made her voice deliberately comforting, as if placating a troubled child. "I'll let her know you were in asking about her, *Mister* Conrad. Would you like an appointment? Mom has an opening on Thursday afternoon at three."

He scowled.

Then he took one step closer, just close enough to breathe on her face. "Just because Mary Bristol likes something or says something, doesn't make it the law in this town, missy."

"Jess," she corrected him, as if misunderstanding the patronizing tone. "Although most folks call me Dr. Bristol." She moved to the door and swung it open, indicating he should precede her. "I'll let her know that you're still up in arms over last night's meeting, although I don't know why. Yet," she added as she pulled the door shut, then locked it securely. "Why would a man who owns a thriving business and a lovely home in the center of the valley be against improvements to the businesses on the main road after a devastating fire? Clearly you have reasons of your own." He wasn't tall for a man, so she was able to look him in the eye without heels, and she took the advantage. "Which makes me wonder what those are, exactly."

"What I do is none of your business. Or his," he added in a snide voice. The jut of his chin indicated Shane and his men working kitty-corner up the road. "Kendrick Creek has no need for outsiders. We did fine before you showed up. We'll do fine once you've gone."

Jess heard his words, but it wasn't the words that seared.

It was the coolness in his expression. The hard stature of his stance. He was a power-hungry man, and he had the money to have undue influence in this small town. Her mother had kept things on an even keel for decades, never letting the power mongers take a firm hold. What would happen with Mary gone?

Jess knew, just by gazing into this man's steely eyes, and so she pretended an agreement she didn't feel. "It has, but even a strong town like this can use a little help from old friends, can't it? Old-fashioned kindness is one of the things Kendrick Creek is known for."

He dropped his shoulders and tried to smile, but it was a wretched kind of thing. "Those are true words."

She caught sight of Shane heading their way. She'd defused the situation for the moment, and she didn't want Shane to reignite Miles's anger. "You have a good night, now, Mr. Conrad." She moved toward her mother's SUV and intercepted Shane. "Stay right here," she whispered to him, tipping her gaze up to his. "And smile at me as if you just stumbled on the prettiest little thing you ever did see."

"No pretense needed, ma'am." He did smile and the twinkle in his eyes underscored the sincerity. "You are all that and more. Is Miles on the warpath?" He kept his voice soft and his eyes on hers as Miles moved two doors up the road to his big, black, muscular SUV.

"Was, and I used my charms—" she rolled her eyes at the expression "—to waylay him, but he's got a bee in his bonnet over the Main Street improvements. Now, why do you suppose that is?" she whispered, keeping her smile sweet, as if flirting with Shane. Then she realized she *was* flirting with Shane. And it felt good. "Still hoping for municipal development on Conrad land?"

"That would be my guess," Shane replied. "Conrad knows I'm on limited time. If he can figure out a way to stonewall us, he fritters away my time and he wins. My prayers are aimed at not letting him win, but he doesn't admit defeat easily, it seems."

He motioned toward the medical office as he reached down and opened Jess's door for her with his other hand. "One thing about working construction. You get a lot of time to talk with God."

He said it in a way that made it sound ridiculously normal. Jess knew it was anything but, otherwise why would so many churches stand empty?

It made little sense, but then she'd rarely met a man in the city with the kind of drive and contentment she saw in Shane.

"Give your mom a hug for me. I'll come by tomorrow if she's feeling better."

"Hopefully. If not, we'll get her some meds that might help make things better. If nothing else, I intend to make this as easy as I can."

"I know you will." Shane reached out and took one of her hands in his. "She's blessed to have you, Jess."

"Don't." She added a look of warning to the stern word. "Sympathy makes me want to curl up and cry, and I don't have time for that. Not now, anyway. I have to lock down my feelings or I won't be able to move forward."

"Nothing wrong with a good cry." He lifted his free hand to her right cheek. "Cleanses the tear ducts."

His kindness drew her forward. Not into his arms, but she leaned her forehead against the chilled fabric of his Carhartt jacket for just a moment, drawing on his strength.

He dropped his cheek to her hat and sighed.

She pulled back. Gazed up at him. "You're too easy to count on, Shane."

"Nothing bad about counting on folks," he replied. "Coming from the lack of it, I can promise you that having support is much nicer."

She'd always had that.

He hadn't. And yet he was quick to offer it, even though she'd been the witness who'd put him behind bars. "Thank you."

He stepped back. "You're welcome."

"Are you heading home?"

"I'm staying on site for another hour. Dev's making supper for the kids. I want this done for Mary," he added, as if it wasn't a huge sacrifice of time. "So the guys and I are going to make sure that happens. Just in case."

Devotion. Focus. Goodness.

Shane brought to mind every Biblical saying she'd been forced to learn as a child. But he wasn't spouting it. He lived it in a show of steadfast devotion, as if it were easy.

It couldn't be. Could it?

And yet, when she was around Shane and her mother, she wondered.

"I hate it here." Jolie locked eyes with Shane from the base of the stairway two hours later. "It's not like home. You're gone all the time. Sam's got Jed to play with, and I'm bored, bored, bored. I want to go home. Now."

Sometimes Sam ignored his sister's edicts. Not tonight. "Well, I like it so far," he declared as he carefully placed cards to add a wing to a house of cards he'd patiently built with Jed before Shane got home. "Mrs. Smith is really nice, she doesn't yell at all the boys and she thinks frogs are cool."

"I'm glad you like the school," Shane told Sam. The eight-year-old hadn't been a fan of his third-grade teacher back in Maryland.

"I love it," declared Sam. "When Mrs. Smith gives you work and you have a question, she doesn't make you feel bad. You know?"

Shane knew, all right. "I get it." He sat and faced Jolie directly. "What's going on, Jo?"

"Nothing. Why does there always have to be something going on?" she demanded. "Why can't it just be that coming down here was a stupid idea and you could have left us back home and you didn't. Isn't that enough?"

"I'm glad Pops brought us."

Sam should have stayed silent. Intent on his card structure, he didn't see the flash in Jolie's eye.

Shane did. He couldn't react quickly enough to stop the inevitable.

A quick series of steps and a flick of her wrist brought the house of cards down.

"Jolie!" Shane pulled her away, but it was too late. The damage was done, and Sam's face—

He stared at the collapsed card house. Quick tears filled his eyes as he jumped up and whirled around, ready to wail on his sister. "Why did you do that? Why did you wreck something so big and beautiful? Why do you always have to ruin things I make?" he demanded. Hands fisted, he wanted to strike her, and the only thing that kept them apart was Shane, doing his least favorite parenting job: refereeing.

"Stupid cards and stupid house and stupid town."

"Jolie. Upstairs. Now." Shane pointed to the stairs. "Go cool off. I'll be up to talk to you after I help your brother."

She stared at him as if wanting to say something, then spun on her heel and stomped up the stairs as hard and loud as she could. When she got to her room, she slammed the door hard. Twice. Because once wouldn't have made her point.

Sammy burst into tears.

Shane hauled him into his arms and sank onto the

thick-cushioned recliner near the woodstove. "I've got you, buddy. I've got you."

"She's mean. She's mean to me, and she's mean to you, and she shouldn't be mean to anybody, Pops. Our mom would be so sad to see her be so mean to everybody." He sobbed and Shane cradled him like he did when they were smaller children.

Jolie didn't let him cradle her anymore. She shied away from affection, keeping her distance, and the rare times when she showed joy, he remembered what a sweet, loving child she'd been. Then they'd lost her mother and she'd slipped into a sad shadow of her former self. He commiserated, but he couldn't allow her to be hurtful. "I'm so sorry, Sam." He grabbed a few tissues from a nearby box. "Can I help you rebuild your house?"

Sammy wiped his face and blew his nose then sighed. "No. I'll just watch something, okay?"

"Sure." Shane clicked on the TV. In nicer weather, he could limit their television time, but there was little Sam could do right now. He handed him the remote. "Here you go, buddy."

Sam didn't look at the pile of cards. He averted his gaze and curled up on the couch. Years ago, he'd sucked his thumb, and even now, when upset, Sam's right hand hovered near his mouth as if longing for old comforts.

So was Shane. Sadly, there were none to be found tonight.

He climbed the stairs to talk to Jolie and tapped on her door. When she didn't answer, he opened it. She sat on her bed, eyes on the window, knees drawn up.

Resignation emanated from her, as if she didn't know how to overcome the sadness and longing that held her hostage. Truth to tell, he didn't know, either.

He took a seat on the edge of the bed. "Do you need more time?"

She scowled and curled up tighter. The children's therapist he'd hired in Maryland had advised him to let her set the timeline during difficult moments or emotional upsets.

Shane wasn't a fan of that. He was a get-it-out-there, solve-the-problem kind of man. But he didn't want to make mistakes with Jolie. He'd made enough with her mother back in the day, so trying to avoid a repeat meant a lot to him. "I know you're unhappy, Jo."

The scowl deepened.

"And I'm sorry about that. But there are folks here who've lost everything and I want to help them. That means staying for a few months and getting things straightened around."

"There are people here who don't even like you!" She turned and pinned him with her gaze. "Some kids at school said you're a thief and shouldn't be back here and that you should pack up your stupid trucks and go back north and take me with you!"

Her words made his heart ache. "They said that?"

She stared at him as a tear stole down her cheek. It was followed by another and then another. "They said it when I was going to lunch and then I couldn't even eat my lunch. And Devlyn made mac and cheese for supper and I don't like it and she said I could have a sandwich but we don't have the right kind of jam."

He reached an arm out around her and this time she didn't shy away. She let the tears slip down her pale cheeks, one after another, not in a stormy torrent like Sam's flash of anger. This was more tragic and harder to fix. Much harder. "I can't fix all the bratty kids in the world, Jolie, but I can step in if you want me to. Talk to the teacher. I'm sorry they said those things. There are still some people who haven't forgiven me for taking that money when I was a kid."

She glared at him, pulled away, folded her arms and tucked her chin.

"Kids echo what they hear at home," he said, "but as things get rebuilt, folks will sing a different tune. They'll see fixed buildings and fresh paint and new sidewalks, and they'll like it. But it's always hard to see that stuff ahead of time."

"So I just have to suffer until then?"

"No." He kept his voice firm. "We have to be patient. I can talk to the teacher and the principal. No one should pester or bully you at school, darlin'."

She sighed and gripped one hand with the other, as if holding back or holding on. Shane wasn't sure which. Then she sighed again. "It'll be okay." She lifted her chin slightly. "I know people need your help. Sometimes I just want to punch people, you know?"

He knew, all right. "And then we turn the other cheek."

"I hate that part."

"I know." He kissed the top of her head.

She sat forward. "I'll go see Sam. And I'll pick up his cards."

"A good start."

She slid off the bed and headed downstairs.

When he followed a few minutes later, the cards were in a neat stack on the table. He motioned to the door. "Sorry about the jam. Let's go make a grocery run so that doesn't happen again."

"Now?"

"Like tonight?" Sammy shifted his attention quickly. "Let's go!"

There weren't any supercenter grocery stores in Kendrick Creek, but he was pretty sure they could find strawberry jelly without chunks and some version of Sammy's favorite breakfast cereal. Because if there was one thing he'd learned about kids, it was that the right foods had a far-reaching effect on daily life.

How he wished healing a broken heart could be as simple.

## Chapter Fourteen

Jess looked up when Shane came into the clinic the next morning and frowned. "What's wrong?"

"Jed's sick."

"Stomach bug?"

The frown deepened. "Yeah."

"And that means Dev can't watch the kids this afternoon," she supposed.

"Exactly. And I don't have any backup babysitting."

"Bring them over to my mother's place." He started to shake his head, but she stopped him with a raised hand. "She's feeling better. I think she may have had a touch of that bug, too, but she was pretty chipper this morning. She's super relieved it wasn't the cancer that made her light-headed and nauseous. I never thought I'd be happy about norovirus; and yet, here we are."

She'd been making notes in file charts on her electronic notebook. She stood and came his way. "Unless there's an emergency, I'm done by four today, just in time for the kids to be dropped off at Mom's. And Mom took chicken out of the freezer, so why don't you guys have supper with us. Okay?"

"Jess, I—"

She wasn't about to entertain some lame excuse when Shane went boldly out of his way to be kind. "So it's all right for you to help others but not let anyone help you? How's that working out for you, by the way?"

Her words made him smile. "You make a good point."

"Always did," she told him. "I found a box of my old books last night. Is Jolie a reader?"

"Voracious."

"Then I'll give them to her tonight. Let's see if we can ease her time here with some oldies but goodies."

Shane met her gaze. "I'd like to find something that helps makes her smile again. That gets rid of that look in her eye every time a doorbell rings or a door opens, like she's hoping and praying her mother will come back. It breaks my heart to see her like this."

"She's suffered two major losses," Jess observed.

Shane seemed confused.

"Her mother and her father. Years apart, but still a notable loss for someone her age. This behavior isn't unusual for a person who's lost both parents. Been there. Done that." She aimed a sympathetic look up at him. "It isn't pretty."

He grimaced. "I never thought of you that way until this moment."

"Which way?" She lifted her brow in question as she poured a fresh cup of coffee and held it out to him. "Coffee?"

"I never say no to coffee." His face relaxed when she handed the first cup to him. "I mean losing your parents. I always thought of you being on the winning side of that deal, because you ended up with the best mom in the county."

"I did," she agreed as she puffed a breath of air over her coffee. "But there's something about being an orphan that leaves a mark. Like, who was my father? Did my biological mother even know who he was?" she asked. "I shy away from DNA testing sites because a part of me doesn't want to find out who I'm related to or that my father was a horrible creature.

"My mother was too busy getting high to take care of me, and no one from the family stepped in to help, so why would I want to know more?" She shrugged and risked a sip of coffee. Still too hot. She set it down and faced Shane. "Kids wonder. They might accept what's going on, but they wonder. And Sam and Jolie are a lot older than I was when my mother died. That kind of thing leaves a mark, so maybe a box of good books will make her smile. Or at least transport her to a new place while you're here."

"Thank you, Jess."

"You're welcome. And you are under strict instructions not to bring me any more fudge tarts."

He frowned, confused. "You used to like them."

"Still do," she admitted. "I ate three of them and only saved one for Mom, so—" She raised her hand to shake a finger at him.

He caught it instead. Studied it. Then her hand. Then

slowly—oh so slowly—he locked eyes with her as he kissed the inside of her wrist.

And then he kissed her.

He didn't hesitate, as if he'd been wanting to kiss Jess for a long, long time. He drew her into his arms and ended the question that had been dancing in her head for over two dozen years. What would it be like to kiss Shane Stone?

He pulled back too soon, sprinkled kisses over her face and her head, then kissed her again. When he was done, he sighed. "I've been wanting to do that since I was eighteen years old, Jess."

"Yeah?"

"Oh, yeah." He leaned in and kissed her again. "And it was positively worth the wait."

He was right. It was. But this couldn't be a casual thing. They had too many responsibilities. Too many people relying on them. "Except there are things in the way, Shane."

He didn't back down, which made him even more appealing. Jess hadn't thought that possible. "A good builder finds a way to solve problems," he replied. "There's always a way to make things work. Some things just take a little more ingenuity than others."

"Ingenuity doesn't fix cancer," she whispered, then rested her head against his chest for too brief a time. "Didn't we just talk about how tough all this is for Sam and Jolie? We can't do anything that makes this worse for them. We're the grown-ups. We understand that timelines aren't always the way we want them to be."

She straightened and took a step back. "Those kids don't need any more surprises in their lives."

She raised her coffee cup. "Here's to good coffee and great friendships." She expected him to touch his cup to hers, a signal of agreement.

He didn't.

He touched her cheek instead, and the feel of his callused hand against her skin felt good and right.

"Jess, I'm putting this where I put all the problems I can't solve with power tools and a hammer. In God's hands. And despite the hills and valleys…" He smiled and pressed his lips to her forehead, making her rethink her stoicism. "Some things are definitely worth fighting for."

He left then, but his warmth and joy lingered after he'd gone. That wasn't an easy thing to shrug off, and if she was honest with herself…

She didn't want to shrug it off at all.

"This is where we're going?" Sammy stretched up from his seat as Shane pulled into Mary's driveway that afternoon. "With the bears and owls and stuff? Cool!"

Sammy's shout of joy made Shane see Mary's cabin through a boy's eyes.

The hillside setting was a Smoky Mountain masterpiece.

Not because it was grandiose. It wasn't. But Mary had positioned the cabin on the hillside, overlooking the valley, and while she'd cleared enough trees for a view, the forest behind it backed right up the mountain.

The stone staircase climbed the hill with purpose, inviting visitors in.

The rooftop dormers created light in a Cape Cod–style shape. The broad front porch invited relaxation on one side and practicality on the other where two face cords of wood stood stacked, ready to burn. A life-sized wooden bear and two cubs marked a garden path at one side, and a carved replica of a barred owl family faced the house from a hollow in a nearby tree.

But there was whimsy, too, something he hadn't noticed on his visits this week. Maybe because it got dark early and stayed dark late, or maybe he just wasn't paying attention. But with the kids, he noticed because everything was different through a child's eyes.

Today's breeze had set the wind chimes in motion, and the high and low notes seemed to soften the cold, wet day, as if offering promises of sweeter, gentler times.

The yard was like the owner, he realized as they opened the car door. Strong and creative. Qualities she'd given to her daughter, as well.

He was going to knock, but Jess opened the door when they drew near. "Come in, that wind bites, doesn't it?"

Sam hurried in. Jolie didn't drag her feet, but she didn't hustle, either, leaving Jess standing with the door ajar. When she got inside, Jess swung the door closed with a quiet click. "This is when a woodstove becomes a homeowner's best friend. Do you guys have homework?"

Sam shook his head. "I did my reading on the bus

and my math paper in school. This teacher is so nice, she gives us fifteen minutes to do our homework at the end if we're good, and we were all good today. So no homework," he explained with a cute grin. "Jed's sick. I think he's like real sick." Sam pretended to throw up.

"Sam. That's rude."

"But accurate," Jess told him. "There's a bug going around."

"Bugs don't make people sick." Jolie didn't fold her arms, but she looked up to meet Jess's gaze. "Bacteria and viruses do. I think most doctors know that."

Shane was about to reprimand her when Jess burst out laughing. "You're one hundred percent correct, and there are some people in New York City who would be so happy to put me in my place, girl, because it is, of course, a virus. Do you know how small viruses are?"

Now Jolie frowned. "How would I know that?"

"Microscope. Computer. Internet searches."

"I don't have anything like that. Well, I have a tablet, so I could look things up."

"Exactly, but if you go look in that room right there—" Jess pointed to her mother's office "—you'll find some cool stuff. When I told Mom you liked science, she thought it might be fun to check out her lab area."

"There's a lab here?"

"Not a real one," said Mary as she came forward from a side room.

Shane breathed a sigh of relief when he saw her because she looked better than the last time he'd been in her presence.

"But I like to study the whys and wherefores of infectious diseases, so I've got examples and slides. Is your homework done?"

Jolie nodded.

"Then come on back."

There was no hesitation in Jolie's step now. She followed Mary into the first-floor office as Jess turned to Sam. "I left the stuff up you guys got out the other day."

Sam grinned. "Our dungeon lives on."

Shane laughed. "I like how you think, kid."

Sam clattered down the stairs. "Can me and Jed play here again? Like soon?"

"When he's better," Jess promised. She turned back to Shane. "Go get your stuff done, *Pops*."

He answered her grin with an over-the-top frown. "They pegged me with that years ago. It stuck."

"Well, I think it's sweet," she told him. "Can you be back for supper at six thirty?"

"How about I bring pizza? Make it easy?"

Mary heard his response and poked her head out of the office. "Chicken and dumplings, snap peas and apple pie. Don't mess with me, Shane."

No smart man argued about chicken and dumplings in Tennessee. "No, ma'am."

Shane headed for the door. "Six thirty, then. And thanks again, Jess. I hope we don't get you sick."

People always worried about sharing germs with a cancer patient or survivor, but Jess had been in medicine a long time. Germs were a constant in life. "It's a kid's prerogative to contaminate things. I'm not immunocompromised now, and Mom's already had it. It's all good. I'm just hoping your crew stays unscathed."

"I'm hoping the same thing," he told her. "The quicker we get things done, the more we can do. When I look at what needs to be done, I realize that twelve weeks is barely a drop in the bucket. But we'll do what we can. See you later." He reached for her hand, and then he didn't let go. He stood there for drawn-out seconds, his gaze locked with hers, then gave her hand a light squeeze before releasing it. When he did let go, the warmth of his touch, his grip, lingered.

# *Chapter Fifteen*

A perfect fit.

That's how Shane felt when Jess was around.

It should have been a ridiculous notion, but it wasn't.
It was right. It felt right. Yet her morning scolding stayed
with him because she'd made a good point. Putting kids
in cancer's crosshairs again wasn't something anyone
should do lightly. But would this timing have happened
if it wasn't of God?

*Bucko, the Bible is full of stories about romances run
amok. You might want to throw up a caution sign here.*

Caution was the last thing he wanted, which meant
the mental warning was right, but his head wasn't in
sync with his heart.

Jess was meant for him. He'd longed for it as a teen,
and he knew it now as a man. If anyone had asked him
if love at first sight could exist, he'd have laughed it off
as impossible.

*Wrong.*

He'd known it the moment their eyes met on that

snowy mountain road a week before, and he knew it now, every time she smiled his way or teased him about something. Her voice called to him. Her scent enveloped him. The very nature of her take-charge personality suited him because he wasn't afraid to take charge of a situation, either.

She'd sent him to jail because doing the right thing meant something to her, then and now. Him, too.

But it wasn't just the past that hogtied him from embracing love at this point in life. It was the future. Hers and Mary's. And Jess's lack of faith, which was such a mainstay to him.

The kids had already lost their mother to cancer. A responsible parent wouldn't put them in that situation again. Sure, stuff happened. Life didn't come with guarantees and setting kids up for grief seemed wrong. But when he was around Jess, the last thing he wanted to do was to walk away.

Which meant that was exactly what he needed to do. The resolve lasted a full five minutes because Pete stopped by the clinic project on his way to the cabins.

"Looks good," he noted when he surveyed their progress.

"It's moving along," Shane answered.

Pete reached up his left hand and pulled the lobe of his ear slightly. If Pete had a tell, that was it. "What's on your mind, Pete?"

"This place."

Shane waited.

"The people," Pete continued. "The town, the damage, the power-hungry guy wanting to mess things up and take charge the minute we leave."

Shane couldn't deny having similar concerns. "Miles is a jerk, but we can't change everything, Pete. You know that."

"Wasn't thinking of changing everything," Pete replied, and it was clear he was choosing his words with care. "But we've got the projects back home nailed down and there's plenty of good help there, and you and I have talked about expanding. Reaching out. Doing more."

Shane stared at him.

"So what if one of us stays here?"

"Why do I feel like Adam and that stupid apple right now?" Shane muttered because the idea of staying here and helping Kendrick Creek, tempted him. "It's impossible, Pete."

"It's not," Pete told him. "Scary, yes. You've got a history here, and that's not always easy, but nothing you can't handle now. I'm not pushing," he added. "But a man working on a broken church has a lot of time to think things through. Maybe God put you here for something more than fixing buildings. Maybe he put you here to fix people, too. Set things right. Something to think on, is all."

Leave the posh suburbs of Maryland and open a branch of Stonefield Construction in Kendrick Creek, Tennessee?

Jess wasn't staying. She'd made that crystal clear. But what if Pete was right? What if God had put Shane here to be more than a quick-fix visitor? But then the kids would have to deal with his and Chrissie's pasts. He ran his fingers through his hair and grimaced. "There's a lot of history here, Pete. Not just mine. Chrissie's. How can I permanently settle her kids into an area that knows so much about her? Jolie's already taking heat because of who I am."

Pete understood Shane's backstory better than most. "Takes fire to make steel," Pete offered. "The strongest folks are the ones that handle the heat, and those kids have you as backup, Shane. That's nothing to shake a stick at. I'm going to stop by Doc's place, say hi to the kids and then head up the hill. Giz made a pot of chili and we're going to go over some figures. I'll send them on to you when we've got it worked out."

These men weren't just working. They were putting in ten- and twelve-hour days, determined to make a difference. How would he ever find a crew like that down here?

Pete must have read his mind because he made his parting shot as he headed for the door. "There are good people everywhere, Shane. The guy that gave us his cabins. Bobby Ray and his demo-moving crew. And a welder stopped by the church today to tell me he'd volunteer his services to put the bell tower back together. Part of the reason you're good folk is because you came from good folk. They just didn't happen to be related to you."

Pete made a great point. Family wasn't necessarily family by blood, especially in Tennessee. They were related by love, and Kendrick Creek was sure showing him a lot of that.

* * *

How could she be surrounded by so much potential sadness and feel this good?

Jess knew the answer without taking time to examine the question as she finished dinner preparations with Shane.

It was him. All him.

Jolie was deep in a book and Sam was building a castle in the downstairs rec room. Her mom was going over the day's notes from the clinic when Shane arrived a few minutes early, tossed off his jacket, noted the set table and moved straight into the kitchen with the words "How can I help?"

Beautiful words. A servant's heart. An amazing man.

The draw to him was strong, as if her heart cried out to his. In all her years of work and excitement in the big city, she had never felt this way, so maybe she wasn't meant for the big city like she'd once thought. Maybe it was more about who she was with, rather than where she lived. "Test that gravy?"

He cooled a spoonful of gravy, tasted it and made a quick pronouncement. "Short on pepper. Can you hand me that pepper grinder?" Shane reached across the island as she sprinkled fresh chopped chives on half of the dumplings.

"Here you go." She handed the grinder over.

His hand touched hers.

Their eyes met, and when he grazed her palm with his fingers—then winked—she wasn't sure if she should flirt back or smack him. "Stop it," she ordered softly, but she didn't mean it, and he seemed to know that right off.

"It's going to be a long few months, Jess."

She couldn't fault his reasoning, but she could counter it with practicality. "Not if I'm seeing patients all day and you're fixing buildings."

"The majority of the buildings are in the vicinity of that clinic," he noted. "I'm pretty sure God plunked me almost next door so's you'd notice me. And it worked."

"I blame the fire," she replied, but then amended her stance. "Although it is weird to have the timing work out like this." She noted her mother with a glance before bringing her attention back to Shane. "Being passed over for the job I'd worked so hard to get and end up as a free agent when my mother needs me most? It's kind of unbelievable, isn't it? I can oversee Mom's practice as needed. This accident of timing has given me the chance to be strong for her, and I'm going to make the most of it."

"It's no accident of timing," he told her in a confident tone. "God's timing."

"Why are good coincidences called God's timing and bad ones are called fate?" she asked, but she didn't give him time to answer because the food was ready. "Hey, guys," she called. "Supper."

Sammy didn't need to be told twice. He raced up the stairs and slid into a chair with all the gusto of a typical eight-year-old boy. "My friend Moira calls it dinner." He made a comic face of disbelief. "I told her it's 'supper,' but she said when her dad takes her mom out on a date, they go to dinner, so that's that. I told her that's just silly."

"And the debate rages on," murmured Mary as she crossed the room. She swept the filled table a look of pure appreciation. "This looks marvelous, Jess and Shane. Thank you so much for finishing it up. And, Jess, you had a busy day at the office, didn't you?"

"Let me just say there wasn't a minute to get bored," Jess told her. "Jenny's a great organizer, she keeps things moving, but a two-person practice will need another hand on deck. Have you thought of tempting a blood lab to set up an office here in town? That would save folks a thirty-minute ride."

"We'd probably need more practitioners on hand to make it worth their while, but it's a great thought," Mary agreed. "It puts patients first. This looks marvelous, Jess." She noted the chicken and dumplings with a look of appreciation. "Thanks for stepping in so I could catch up on files."

"It smells like that old-fashioned diner we go to, Pops." Jolie came forward. She hadn't set the book down. She'd brought it to the table and held it up for Shane to see. "From Jess. A whole collection she had. It's a really good mystery."

"And you love mysteries."

"I do," she admitted. "Can we come here tomorrow, too?" she asked as she sat. "If Jed's not better? Doc Mary has cool slides to examine in her office. Bug legs and antennae and blood spots."

"While that sounds like a real good time—" his expression suggested otherwise "—it's up to Mary and

Jess," he told her. "Devlyn texted that she'd need one more day, but I don't want to impose. I can duck out of work—"

"One of us can wrap up early," Mary assured him. "It will feel good to be back in the office, seeing patients, so maybe we can cut Jess loose to meet the kids here. And, honestly, if Devlyn ever wants to bring the kids here to check things out, she's welcome. There can't be a lot to do at your rental, and Jed's toys, well..." She said no more but they all knew what had happened to Jed's toys. "The woods are perfect for science lessons in the spring. Unless you wake up a very hungry, or-nery bear," she teased with a look at Sam.

"But they're sleeping now. Right?" His expression begged assurance. Just in case.

"For the moment," she told him, laughing.

It felt good to hear her mother laugh.

It was a family meal.

The last time Jess had enjoyed a family meal at a big table was when her friend Ashley had invited her to their cramped Brooklyn apartment to tell her she and her family were moving to the heartland.

Their choice surprised her. They had great jobs in Lower Manhattan, lived in a classic neighborhood in Park Slope, and had all the amenities a thriving city could offer.

But their move had helped spur Jess's awareness and now here she was, surrounded by people, a home-cooked dinner—supper, she corrected herself with an inner smile. Embraced by the mountains she used to call home. She could breathe here. She could think. It surprised her that she'd barely noticed the frantic pace she'd kept up in the city until she got here and had time to talk with patients. Watch them and their reactions. Sense their needs.

Practicing medicine was different here.

But so was she. Jess was beginning to think that might be a good thing.

Sammy threw his arms around Jess and gave her a big hug as Shane and the kids readied to leave a half hour later. "This was so fun!" he hooted. "Your downstairs is like the best ever I like it so much!" He spread his arms wide, his expression hopeful.

"If Devlyn wants to bring you guys over here to play, you're welcome anytime," Mary told him. "I'll text her and let her know."

"Awesome!" Sammy didn't barrel into Mary. He grinned at her, flashing his bigger front teeth. "See you tomorrow!"

He charged out the door. Shane caught the old-fashioned wooden storm door before it banged shut. "He's all boy."

"Just the way he should be," noted Jess.

Jolie had reorganized the box of books. Mysteries on one side, regular fiction on the other. She came forward and Shane reached out for the box. "I can carry them, honey."

"I've got them. But thank you." She offered him a quiet look. "You always help me, Pops, but it's good for me to learn how to take care of myself. I'm ten now."

Shane winced but Jolie didn't see it. She'd turned toward Jess. "Thank you for this. I'll have so much fun reading them."

"Good." Jess didn't mention that the girl's expression belied her words, or that her somber bearing was tough to watch. She touched a hand to Jolie's shoulder. "I buried myself in books when I was a kid, right through high school. I loved reading, loved transporting myself to other worlds, other times, other characters. And these are some of my favorites."

"I'll take real good care of them."

"Thank you." Should she hug her?

That would mess up Jolie's need for space. Her burdens stood in sharp contrast to Sam's easygoing manner. "I'll see you tomorrow, all right?"

"Yes." Shane held the door wide, and Jolie balanced the box. It was a struggle, and still she didn't ask for help.

Jess turned back to Shane. Her mother had gone upstairs. She motioned toward his truck. "They're good kids, Shane. Sam's a riot and Jolie's got an old soul, but she'll be all right."

"You think?" Worry lines creased his brow.

"Give it time," she reminded him. "It's not just about loss, it's a combination of maturity, loss, change and a dose of self-doubt."

"Why would a beautiful, straight-A student doubt anything?" Shane wasn't pretending his surprise. "How can that be something?"

"Maybe because it isn't enough." Saying the words, Jess realized their truth. Not just for Jolie, but for herself. She'd been trying to be top dog for as long as she could remember and, in the end, what had she gained?

Nothing of note. And that was sad.

He gave her a tender smile. Then he hooked a thumb at the truck. "Gotta go." He pushed open the door.

"I know. I'm glad we all had supper together, Shane."

"Me, too. It was perfect, Jess."

The warmth in his gaze made her blush because it wasn't "perfect." A sad child, a cancer survivor and a cancer patient?

And yet it felt right, so she went along with his assertion. "It was, wasn't it?" She leaned up and feathered a kiss to his cheek, just because. "Maybe perfect isn't about the numbers, Shane. Maybe it just comes down to the people."

"Pops, it's cold out here! Like freezing cold!" Sam's plea for warmth pulled Shane away, but as she watched his black truck pull out of the driveway, a hint of peace settled in. But it was false hope. Shane would leave and her mother would be gone, leaving what?

*You know what. People in need. Sick people, everyday folks wanting and needing what your mother gave them for over forty-five years. Solid medical care.*

The thought of such a major change made her hands tremble. She'd come here wanting to help, not wanting to step into her mother's shoes. So why did working at the makeshift clinic feel right?

A light blinked on in the town below. The steeple light from the church, broken in the fire, now cast a golden glow in four directions, begging to be noticed. She'd trudged by so many beautiful and historic

churches in New York—a mainstay along the streets
of Manhattan. But the magnificent cathedrals didn't
call to her.

This humble church did.

Mary came downstairs as Jess closed the thick inner
door. "They're off?"

"Yes. How was your call with Ed and Hassie?"

Mary settled into the corner of the couch. She'd lost
the wan look that spiked Jess's worry. She was tired,
but she'd perked up once the stomach bug had run its
course. "They want help finding a home for the grand-
daughters before the county steps in and does it for
them."

"That's a courageous step." Jess didn't take the seat
beside her mother. She sank to the floor alongside her
instead. "How brave of them to make that choice. And
if you need time to scope things out, I'll be here as long
as you need me. Okay?"

Mary reached out a hand to Jess's cheek. "I don't
know what I'd do without you."

"Well, the feeling's mutual, so if you could arrange
not to die, that would be a help."

"I know." Mary smiled, but it was full of regret. "If
I could, I would, but my body and the Lord have other
plans, it seems."

"I looked into possible treatments," Jess admitted.
"At lunch today." She turned to face her mother. "I
wanted to buy you some time. Then I figured I'd better
talk to you because I'm sure you've already checked."
She put her hand over her mother's in a compassion-

ate gesture. "Not to talk you into anything, but to see what's out there."

"Thank you, Jess." Mary kept her hand along Jess's cheek, the way she used to when Jess was a little girl. "We did the tests in Houston. The recommended chemos weren't an option for me. I've got the AGT factor, so surgery and radiation were the best shots at giving me time, and they did. Time enough to be here now. To have you here, and fix what we can."

That was how her mother had kept her treatment under the radar. "No chemo, no hair loss."

"And no tissue damage from radiation, so I could continue practicing, but that's got to come to an end soon," Mary said softly. "I can't risk making a bad judgment call. The confusion is likely to grow and fatigue will become an issue."

"Hence the dolled-up practice to lure new doctors in."

"God may have closed some doors with that fire, but he left windows open, and this town deserves a chance to shine," Mary told her. "It's never had the opportunity.

"That fire took a lot, but if we're smart, we can rise up like that bird." She frowned, searching for a word that should have come to her instantly.

It pained Jess that it didn't.

"The phoenix," Jess supplied.

"Yes." Mary offered a rueful look. "It used to be me helping you remember things."

"So now we switch things up a little." Jess squeezed her hand lightly. "No regrets, no worries."

"There's not a moment of raising you that I've forgotten or regretted," Mary replied. "Except when I said no to that blue-and-green prom dress," she amended.

"In retrospect, it was hideous, so thank you for standing your ground." Jess clutched her mother's hand. "We did okay, didn't we?"

"Then and now," Mary told her. She yawned and laid her head back on the thick pillow Jess had brought down from upstairs the day before. She yawned again as weariness took over. "Good night, my darling."

An endearment that Jess hadn't heard in person for far too long. "Good night, Mom. I love you."

A faint smile softened Mary's jaw. "I know, honey. You always have. We make a good team, Jess."

They did.

The thought that Mary would no longer be part of the team made Jess's eyes water. She wanted to reply, to agree, but the words wouldn't form around the lump in her throat.

"No need for words, darling," Mary whispered. "Not between us. You go rest, all right?"

Mary's eyes drifted closed again.

Jess crept up the stairs. The waxing January moon shone like a smiley face outside her window, a crescent set aloft in a shimmer of stars. She couldn't even remember the last time she noticed a moonrise. And yet here was the moon, glimmering in the western sky, a reminder that it hadn't moved.

She had.

Jess curled up in her mother's bed and this time didn't fight the tears. She let them come, unchecked.

For her, for her mother, for sorrowed children, and for all the sadness she'd seen over the years.

And when she finally blotted her eyes, calmed her aching chest and blew her nose, the moon still shone, a curve of gentle, reflective light.

She wiped her eyes one more time then spotted the wall hanging a patient had given Mary years ago. *"Weeping may endure for a night..."* it read along the top rows, then below, in a prettier font it said, *"but joy cometh in the morning."*

One of her mother's favorite verses.

She took a breath. A deep one. She glanced at the moon, then read the verse one more time. And then she laid down her head and went to sleep.

## Chapter Sixteen

Nearly a dozen years of medical training and over a dozen more in experiential learning didn't top Sam's and Jolie's grins when Jess handed them a box of brownie mix and let them make brownies the next afternoon.

"Why are we making these? Is it something special?" wondered Jolie as she measured the oil into the bowl while Sam cracked the eggs.

"We're celebrating that we've escaped the stomach bug so far," Jess told them. "In medical circles, that's a big deal."

"Then hooray for us!" Sam poured the cracked eggs into a bowl as he whooped, and his excitement caused one slippery egg to cascade outside the bowl and onto the island countertop. "Oh, no!" He looked chagrined. "Miss Jess, I'm so sorry!"

"Accidents happen, Sam," she began, but Jolie's reaction claimed center stage.

"What is the matter with you?" Voice low, she slipped off the stool and faced her little brother. "Why can't you just get things right? Do things right? Is it so hard to put eggs in a bowl, Sam? Like a normal person?"

"Jolie." Jess put a hand on her shoulder. "Stop. It's not a big deal. It's just an egg."

"I'm sorry." Dismay darkened Sam's features. "I shouldn'a got so excited, and now I messed things up. I'm sorry, Miss Jess."

"Sam." She bent to face him as Jolie stalked off, plunked herself onto the couch and put a sofa pillow over her face. "We all make mistakes. Kids and grown-ups. It's all right. Here." She handed him a folded paper towel. "Slide that bad boy into this bowl. We'll toss it away and crack a new one, okay?"

"Just slide it?"

"This is where we use their slipperiness to our advantage," Jess assured him while she wet a dishcloth to wash the countertop. And when she'd washed and dried it, she handed him another egg. "If at first you don't succeed, try, try again."

"Pops says that, too." He cracked the egg and used a less excited approach to let it slide into the mixing bowl. "He says we've gotta keep on trying, but JoJo gets mad when I mess up because she thinks our dad won't want us if I keep messing up. Our real dad," he added to make sure Jess understood, and she did. The little boy's words made her heart stand still.

"Stop talking!" Jolie jumped up, eyes wide. A flood of emotions rained across her sweet face. "Why do you have to say things, Sam? You're such a baby!"

"I'm not," he protested right back. "I'm just saying what you told me, how our real dad might not find us

down here because he might not know where we a
It's not a secret. Right?"

Jolie's face crumpled. Clearly it *had* been a secr

And Sam, so excited about making brownies n
ments before, sat on the stool, utterly defeated.

Jess stood in the middle, having no idea how to
hearts torn in two by emotional trauma.

A thought nudged her as she watched Jolie's sho
ders shake with quiet tears.

*You know exactly how because you wondered*
*same thing.*

Jess crossed the room and took the seat next to Jo

Jolie turned away, tucking her head, wanting som
thing she couldn't have and would maybe never ha
the love of biological parents. And that was somethi
Jess could understand. "I don't know who my fatl
is," she began softly. Sam didn't move. He sat on t
stool, looking bereft. Head buried in the pillow, Jo
stayed turned away.

"When I was two years old, my mother and my a
decided to take a drunken drive across the mounta
They put me in the back seat of the car with no car s
and no seat belt. No booster seat. I was just sitting ba
there when we ended up in a terrible accident."

Compassion brought Sam her way. "Were you hur

She nodded. "Seriously hurt. My head, my legs, n
pelvis. I was like a broken doll, lying in the woo
when Doc Mary found me. She heard the ambular
call on her scanner." Jess pointed out a newer versi
of the scanner on Mary's counter. "She got to me ev
before the ambulance and made sure they took me

the closest hospital first to get me stable, then to the best one.

"And every day she'd be here in Kendrick Creek saving lives and helping kids and getting folks healthy, and every single night she'd drive all the way to that hospital in Knoxville to spend time with me. Hold me. Sing to me.

"For a long time I couldn't make sense of anything, because I was hurt so badly, but I can still remember smelling her." She smiled and touched the pillow Jolie clutched. "Vanilla and cinnamon, like an old-fashioned cookie. And I remember her singing to me. Not the words," she told them. "But the tunes, the feeling of being cradled. Later I realized why that felt so good." She met Sammy's gaze with a sad smile. "Because no one had ever cradled me or sung to me before."

"But she did."

"Yes. And then she adopted me and brought me home and made sure I had all the therapy I needed to get better because she loved me so much. It didn't matter that we weren't related, or that I had a different father and mother. It just mattered that she loved me."

"Like our mom loved us," said Sam softly. "And like Pops loves us."

Jess nodded but stayed quiet because this wasn't a contest between Shane and their father. This was a yearning for the person who should love you best to step up to the plate, and their biological father hadn't done that in years.

"I sent him a letter." Jolie whispered the words into the pillow. "I found an old piece of mail from a long time ago and I wrote him a letter to tell him our mom had died and we missed him."

"I don't miss him." Sam's honesty brought Jolie's chin up slightly. "I don't even know him. I miss my mom and I wish she didn't die because she snuggled me every single night," he went on. "Pops does that now, and it's nice, but it's different. But I don't want another dad," he finished honestly. "Because I've got Pops."

Jolie's chin quivered. She didn't look at Sam. She stared beyond him, as if hoping for someone to appear, and Jess laid her hand on Jolie's arm. "But this isn't about Pops, is it, darling?"

Jolie darted a glance her way.

"You know Shane loves you. He's stood by you all along, like Doc Mary did for me, but there's that little part inside us that wants to know why our father or mother doesn't want us. And in the end, Jolie, sometimes there are just no answers to that, and that's when we celebrate the people who *do* love us. Who care for us, who shrug off our mistakes, who gather us in, who set the good example. Because in the end, it's the love that matters. Not the biology."

Knuckles strained white, Jolie clutched the pillow. She didn't look at Jess. Or at Sam. Eyes forward, she made the whole thing clear. "I just don't know why someone wouldn't want their own little boy. Or little girl. But maybe when you have a different family, the old one doesn't matter so much." Her lower lip trembled. "When I read a book about a happy family, I want to be that family. With a mom and a dad and maybe a scooter. And books. Lots of books." She sighed, still looking ahead.

Sam moved forward. "I think about that, too," he whispered. "When I think about how Mom won't ever see me play soccer or go fishing or make the best card towers ever. And then I wonder if she'll see us from Heaven. No one knows, and I think what a sad thing if you can't even see your own little kids from Heaven. So how can it be happy up there? But Pops told me God's way is smarter than even the smartest person and that He's got different things, different ways. And that God will get it right, even if we get sick and our bodies get it wrong."

The simplicity of Shane's explanation to the boy touched Jess. He believed in the will of God but understood the frailty of a mortal life.

"He loves you."

Sam nodded and drew closer to Jess's side. "He always says that. A lot. And maybe I don't even want to meet a different dad because maybe I've got the best one ever." He spoke to Jess, but his eyes searched Jolie's reaction.

Jolie stared forward for a few more seconds. Then, slowly, her fingers loosened their grip on the pillow. She looked at Sam and sighed. "I love Pops, too," she whispered. Her voice caught on the words, but she went on. "I just thought in my head that if our very own dad found out that Mom died, he'd come to rescue us."

"Like a hero."

Her eyes met Jess's. "Yes."

"But maybe it's the everyday heroes we have in our

lives that are the best," said Jess. "The ones we don't notice because they never make us wait."

A shadow lifted from Jolie's gaze. "Because they love us every day. No matter what."

"No matter what." This time Jess reached out and hugged the girl, and Jolie let her. And when she was done, she gestured to the kitchen. "Baking therapy is key," she told both kids. "There's something about creating wonderful food that makes the day shine brighter, and those brownies aren't about to make themselves. You in?"

Sam nodded quickly. "I'm in!"

Jolie wasn't as fast, but she set the pillow down after a few seconds. "Can we add chocolate chips?"

"If Mom's got some, we can add them," Jess promised. She stood and when Jolie took the hand Jess offered, her touch meant something more than fancy titles and big offices. It meant love and trust, and Jess realized nothing could be better than that.

Jolie was trying to find her father.

Jess's quiet text had knocked Shane for a loop because he knew Rod Sauer. The guy was a jerk and a deserter, but he'd kept his opinions to himself for years because why spoil a kid's image of their parent? That seemed petty because actions would speak for themselves.

But he'd just realized that kids were different. Jolie's active imagination had put Rod on a much higher pedestal than the guy deserved, but how could Shane make that clear and not be a jerk himself?

And should he bring this up or let Jolie approach him? The question was answered later that evening. Sam had fallen asleep on the couch and Shane had carried him up to bed. When he came down, Jolie was perched on the edge of the sofa, waiting.

He pulled a small chair up and took a seat. "What's up, darlin'? Can't sleep?"

His usual prescription for sleeplessness was cocoa and a story, but the kids had mostly outgrown bedtime stories.

Jolie stood. She wrung her hands then took a deep breath. "I wrote to my father."

"Oo…kay." He dragged out the word, waiting for more. A mixture of penitence and confusion shadowed her face, but she clearly had something to say and intended to say it. Shane hunched forward, listening.

"I did it last summer," she confessed.

That long ago? And not a word. Shane watched her struggle, at a loss for how to help because Rod had made it clear that he'd wanted nothing to do with his wife or kids. Ever. But that wasn't information Shane or Chrissie had wanted to share with two beloved children.

"I kept waiting for him to come see us." Her voice went soft. "I figured when he realized that Mommy was in Heaven, that he'd want to see us. At least visit us," she added, as if explaining it more to herself than to him. "Not because I didn't love you," she declared, worry drawing her brows together. "I love you so much, Pops. And it wasn't even that I wanted to leave you, it was just wanting my mom or my dad to be around and love me. Love us," she added with a glance toward the stairs.

"Have you heard from him?" Shane asked. He didn't mention that Rod had signed off rights to the kids years ago, leaving Shane free to adopt them when Chrissie passed away.

She shook her head. "I waited and waited and kept watching. I thought he'd write to us."

Her pinched face underscored the anguish of no contact.

"Then I thought maybe the address was wrong, so I looked him up on Nettie's computer."

"While I applaud your resourcefulness, you know that there's a lot of stuff on the internet that's dangerous for children, honey. You could have stumbled into some rough stuff," he reminded her.

"I know, but we saw a mystery thing on TV and that's what they did. They just typed a name and a city into the search thing and found the person."

"So you found him?"

Jolie breathed deeply and nodded. "I wrote to the new address and told him we were with you, that Mom was gone, and I gave him our address and told him I wanted to see him again. I kept hoping he'd show up for my birthday."

Jolie had turned ten in October.

"And then I thought maybe Christmas."

Of course, there'd been no visit or communication, so another disappointment. No wonder she'd seemed so glum with the holidays. He'd assumed it was memories of her mother weighing her down. The empty seat at the table. But it was the other empty seat, and he'd never given that a thought.

"Jolie, I'm sorry." He reached out for her, but she stood just far enough away to maintain her distance.

"I made Sammy promise not to tell."

"He knows?"

"Yes. But he didn't care, Pops. Not like I did, and I don't even know why I cared so much." Her hands fisted as she fought tears. "I think I just wanted to be normal, like kids in storybooks, and then we had to come here real quick and I just kept thinking that maybe he was up there, in Maryland, looking for us and couldn't find us and it made him sad. Or he thought I was a liar or something. And I don't ever tell lies, Pops. You know that."

"Oh, darlin'." He tugged her into his arms, even if she didn't want it, because her pain was his pain. "Not everyone loves being a parent, Jolie. It's weird, but it's true, and sometimes folks don't realize that until after they've already got kids. So maybe that's what happened with your dad."

"Except he's got a little boy."

Shane had to work double time to shove down the anger that rose in his throat.

"I saw a picture of him with my dad and a lady, and they looked happy. So then I thought maybe it was just us he didn't like."

How could he tell this beautiful, amazing child that her father would probably do the same thing to this new family at the first sign of trouble?

He couldn't. "I count my blessings every day, JoJo." The use of her old nickname inspired a thin smile. "And right there at the top of the list is you and your brother. You make the long days of working worthwhile. When

I look at you and see your mama's smile and her pretty golden hair, I realize that while my sister is in God's arms, I've got the most perfect parts of her right here with me. Her children.

"So don't ever think that I don't love you as much as anyone could, honey. You and Sam mean the world to me. But if you want me to help track down your father and make contact with him, I will." He met and held her gaze deliberately. "I don't know what the outcome will be, but I'd do it for you, Jolie. Anytime."

She leaned into him then.

The distance created over the last six months dissolved in one honest conversation. She leaned against him and let him hold her. Talk to her. Parent her. And when he handed her a clutch of tissues from the nearby box, she snuffled, blew her nose and snuffled again. "I'm sorry, Pops."

"For wanting to be loved?"

She frowned. "I guess."

"Nothing to apologize for there, darlin'." He snugged her close and stroked her hair. "We all want to be loved. Every last one of us."

"But what about when people leave?"

He thrust a brow up and waited.

"Maybe I'm just tired of saying goodbye to people. Like loving them and having them leave. It's like I don't even know if I want to love people anymore, you know?"

He bit back a sigh because Jess had nailed this completely, a combination of loss, fear and immaturity.

He held her close. "I know, honey. I know. No one wants to say goodbye to someone they love."

She sighed against his chest, and that sigh punctuated the decision he had to make. Sam and Jolie had seen enough loss in their young lives. Its impact had hit Jolie hard, so how could he put them right back in harm's way with Jess and her mom?

He couldn't.

But that didn't make the decision any easier because the last thing he wanted to do was to give Jess up again. And yet it was the only choice a loving father would dare to make.

# Chapter Seventeen

Twelve very long days.

That's how long it had been since Jess had seen Shane other than from a distance across the road.

She'd been busy, sure. And he was swamped with work. But she was right across the street. If he wanted to stop by to see her, he could.

That could only mean one thing: he didn't want to.

It wasn't easy to shove that thought aside, but she had no other choice. Flu season had resurged once the kids were back in school, and though Kendrick Creek wasn't a big community, one doctor could only do so much. That meant she was working extra hard to keep Mary out of the office and away from germs. No way did she want her immune-compromised mother to catch any wild viral germs, so she'd put Mary on strict lockdown and had taken over the clinic.

And after sitting out the previous year's pandemic, it felt good to be at the helm this year. As long as she didn't think too much about Shane across the street.

Sunday afternoon loomed long and empty. Mary was resting, and Jess was pretty sure she was going to go stir crazy if she sat one more hour in the cozy house. She crossed the room, grabbed her jacket and scarf, and slipped out the front door.

Cold, crisp mountain air made her breathe deep.

The air felt good. The cold felt good, too. It was a clean cold, unsullied by crowds and traffic and packed trains. She started for the road as Devlyn's car turned into the drive. She took one look at Jess as she turned off the car. "Walking?"

"Yes."

"Can I come with? Jed's over at Shane's place and I thought I'd come pester you and your mom."

Jess hadn't realized how much she wanted someone else's company until Devlyn made the offer. "I'd love that, Dev."

"It's fairly pleasant for January, I'll say that," Devlyn began as she fell into step going down the extended driveway. "I view January and February as months to get through, then March comes along with just enough tease and promise to make me breathe full again. Around the middle of the month, anyway."

"It's chilly until mid-April in Manhattan," noted Jess. "We get a few nice days here and there, but if you miss them because you were working a double or sleeping after a double, you might wait a couple of weeks for the next one."

"I can't even." Devlyn made a face of disbelief. "I like my warm weather, Jess. But I expect the city is fun."

It had been. She'd loved it for a long time. It had

suited her, and she wasn't sure when that had stopped being the case, but knew it was before her cancer diagnosis. So why hadn't she ducked out sooner?

She knew why now. Being here had opened her eyes, and maybe her heart. She'd been so focused on the top rung that she hadn't paid attention to the climb. A foolish mistake on her part. "It used to be, but I realized I was ready to move on even before they gave my job away to someone less qualified and not sick."

"Oh. Ouch."

"And my headhunter—"

"Excuse me?"

"A job recruiter."

"Ah. Got it."

"She sent my resumé to some great hospitals. Cleveland, Baltimore and Pittsburgh," she listed, but Devlyn interrupted her.

"The South doesn't need great doctors?" It was the same question Mary had posed weeks before. "Because I'm pretty sure we do."

"Emory and Duke are on the list, too."

"So you're leaving? For sure?"

"Eventually, yes." The sadness in Devlyn's voice thinned Jess's resolve. "That's always been the plan."

"I know, Jess." Devlyn walked alongside her as they turned toward town. "From the time you were a kid, you loved the idea of big cities and crazy traffic." Devlyn sighed, then shoulder-nudged Jess good-naturedly. "Ignore me. It's just been nice having you and Shane back. A part of me remembered how things used to be and I got all nostalgic."

Nostalgic for Kendrick Creek?

Jess would have scoffed at that notion a few weeks ago. Not now.

"I hoped you'd take over Mary's practice and teach us all how to be better versions of ourselves."

"This coming from a woman with a bumper sticker that says 'We don't care how they do it in New York.'" Jess sent her an amused look.

"That came with the car, although it's not an uncommon sentiment. How soon will you be leaving?"

Jess chose her answer carefully. "Waiting on interviews."

"And Mary's health."

Jess winced. "She thinks it's a secret."

Devlyn tucked her arm through Jess's, like they used to do as girls. "I know. She likes her privacy, but a woman who never takes a vacation left for nearly three weeks last winter. That was my red flag, and I saw her fatigue at the fire. She kept going because that's who she is, but I saw it. Is it bad, Jess?"

Jess nodded.

Devlyn squeezed her arm lightly before letting go. "Then thank you for stepping in. She's a cornerstone for this town. And whatever happens, I'll be forever grateful for her wisdom and dedication. She stood by me when I lost my parents. And when I discovered I was pregnant with no marriage prospects, she was the rock I leaned on. I love her, Jess."

"Me, too. Stupid cancer. It messes up so much. Even things it shouldn't," Jess added.

"Will being a cancer survivor be a factor in finding

a job? A highly skilled doctor like you?" Disbelief colored Devlyn's voice. "That's unbelievable."

She'd always been able to count on Devlyn's honesty, even when it stung, like now. "Not legally, but probably. It's messed up health, work, and—" She paused before she said too much.

"Shane."

Before Jess could deny her feelings about Shane, Devlyn held up a hand. "Save your breath, it was obvious from the first time I saw the two of you together and if you both weren't so amazingly stubborn and a little stupid, it would be movie-worthy."

"I like movies where the heroine saves herself and the hero is impressed by her strength and fortitude and comes along for the ride."

"Why deny yourselves a chance to see where this could go?" she asked. "Why not give it a try? Haven't the two of you been through enough?"

"Exactly why we can't pursue this," Jess said softly. "Chrissie's kids don't need another cancer patient around. You know that, Dev. Adults don't put kids in the middle of a tough situation."

"Except that life hands us rough roads on a regular basis," reasoned Devlyn. "You know how sacrificial Shane is. His love language is to sacrifice for others."

Jess frowned. "I don't think he'd consider taking over with the kids to be a sacrifice. More like an honor, especially considering his troubles in the past."

Devlyn stopped as they neared the church. The road was quiet, a gentle snowfall adding a layer of white to tree branches and yards. Few stores were open for the next six weeks, a winter lull. She stared at Jess then frowned. "Mary never told you."

"Told me what?"

"About Shane."

Jess faced her, puzzled. "I don't know what you're talking about."

"I see that, and to me it's so obvious because it's just who he is, who he always was. But, Jess…" Devlyn hesitated, took a deep breath and went on. "Shane didn't steal that money. He never stole anything. He would never do that."

Shane hadn't taken the money?

Jess looked at her. Really looked. And then—

Then she had a light-bulb moment. A glimpse of clarity she'd never considered because she'd been so busy assessing right versus wrong. "Chrissie."

"Yes."

Her heart paused. Literally. And when it started beating again, an ice-cold chill raced down her back. She pulled her jacket closer, but it did nothing to ward off the shiver. "He went to prison for her."

"And never said a word." Devlyn continued, "He thought no one knew, but anyone who knew them had it figured out. Despite that, there was nothing to be done. They had your eyewitness report and Shane's confession. They had everything they needed. But folks talk, and there're a few of us that know what went down that day. That makes his coming back here to help fix things so much better."

Oh, Shane.

What he'd done. What he'd endured. What he'd confessed to, to give his sister a chance. Thoughts whirled in Jess's head like the snowflakes dancing on today's light breeze. "No one does things like that, Devlyn."

"A man of faith does."

His faith.

Shane didn't hide his belief in God. He wore it with honor, the way he did so many things. To go to prison to protect his sister was an amazing sacrifice. "I put an innocent man in prison."

"Because he let you," Devlyn noted. "He wanted Chrissie to have the chance to begin again, and she did. His sacrifice inspired her to be a better person."

It all seemed so clear now.

Why hadn't she seen that back then?

Jess knew why. She'd been so bitterly disappointed to see the boy she'd been crushing on for almost a year do something so wrong, as if his choice had ruined a coddled girl's dream. How utterly selfish was that?

"Get over yourself," Devlyn advised. "You were sixteen and pretty self-righteous. You're all grown up now, and so is he, so that brings me back to the question of why not give it a shot?" She stopped walking and faced Jess. "God only hands out so many chances."

"But the kids—"

"That part's up to him. There's only so much we can protect kids from, and no one knows what your prognosis really is, correct?"

"It's fairly good, actually."

"So why not run with it, Jess? Because none of us can see the future. Everything we do has risk but it's also got reward, and this could be the best reward of all."

In front of them stood the remnants of the town. The burned buildings had been removed, leaving bare patches, but new buildings would rise up over the coming months. To their left stood the humble white church, glowing softly in the shadow of a cloudy January afternoon. Ground-level floodlights bathed an old-fashioned outdoor nativity scene in the fading light. "Pastor said he was leaving the Holy Family statues up a little longer this year," Devlyn said. "He said seeing it gives people hope, because if ever a family had to deal with anxiety and discord, it was this one."

Like Shane had dealt with growing up, and still had the faith and strength to stand tall and save his sister.

Jess's heart swelled, gazing at the amazing mark Shane had already left on this town. He hadn't just brought expertise and helpful hands. He'd brought hope, not just to her mother's medical practice, but throughout the town. It wasn't just construction she was seeing.

She saw the work of one man. His strength. His sacrifice. His ethic. A trio of qualities that fit her.

Was Devlyn right? Should they give this a chance?

There was only one way to find out. Shane's kids were home tonight, so she'd wait until tomorrow, but one way or another, Jess was determined to have her say.

And like it or not, he was going to listen.

No one who's been in jail ever wants to feel locked up, but that's exactly how Shane's enforced separation from Jess felt.

Sammy had finished a weekend geography assignment after no small amount of coaxing and threats. Jolie was working on a writing project with a greater sense of satisfaction while Shane adjusted figures for current projects in town and a few on the outskirts that had been waiting.

Jolie came by after grabbing a glass of juice and peered over his shoulder, more relaxed now than she'd been in months, which was something to be grateful for. "You're good at math, Pops."

"Well, thank you." He smiled at her. "I want to make sure we're going into each project with the right figures and materials. I hate leaving jobs half done, but we need to finish what we can to get you guys back home where you belong."

"Did the lumber guy really donate a bunch of stuff?" she asked. "That's what Melly Brown said at church this morning."

"He sure did." The owner of Creekside Lumber had come on board in a big way this past week. "He's happy to see improvements in so many places, and he's lived here all his life, and his parents, too. So he wanted to give back to the community."

"You and Mom lived here, too."

He'd steered clear of conversations about the deep past for obvious reasons, but he nodded. "Yes."

"And my grandparents. Right? Even if they weren't really awesome people."

Shane's hesitation pushed her to say more.

"Mom told me about them," Jolie explained. She leaned her elbows on the table and put her chin in her hands. "About how your dad left and your mom wasn't good to you guys and you tried to take care of Mom when she was a kid."

He sat back slightly. "I didn't know she shared that with you. It's kind of rough stuff, Jolie."

She made a face. "Lots of people go through rough stuff, right? You told us that it's not the stuff that makes us, it's how we make ourselves."

He nodded. "But even cool people can make mistakes," he told her. "And then move on from them. That's part of why we came down here to help the town. A lot of these folks looked out for us when your mom and I were young. Now it's my turn."

"And maybe show them you ended up doing all right."

He couldn't deny there was a measure of pride in overcoming a tough beginning and a felony conviction. "Sometimes I wish you weren't so smart, kid."

"I wish Mom was here."

Whoa. Jolie rarely referenced her loss. When she did, Shane perked up and listened. "Me, too. I miss her a lot."

Jolie regarded him with a thoughtful gaze, then totally blindsided him. "If Mom was here, she'd tell people the truth, Pops."

He met her gaze with a look of complete but contrived puzzlement. "About what?"

She put her arms around his neck and hugged him. "You know what, Pops," she whispered. "Sammy doesn't know, she said he was too little to understand, but that we should tell him when he gets bigger. She told me when she got so sick. That she took a lot of money to make it into a gang because she didn't like herself or her life, and that you pretended you did it and went to jail for her."

The tightness in his throat kept him silent for a moment. He pulled back and gazed into Jolie's pretty brown eyes. Her mother's eyes.

"She told me because she didn't want us to grow up thinking you were a criminal. That's all."

That's all?

Adrenaline buzzed through his system. For a moment, he couldn't talk, and could barely breathe.

Chrissie had wanted to tell the kids two years ago, but he'd advised against it. Why mess things up when everything had eventually worked out? Their father had walked away before Chrissie had gotten sick and Shane had been a mainstay in their lives since they'd been born. He'd seen no reason to malign his sister's name after she'd worked so hard to be not just a good person, but a great person.

*Isn't that exactly why?* his conscience asked. *Because being a great person means taking responsibility for your actions. For your life. And that's what Chrissie did.*

"I won't tell Sam," she promised. "We can tell him when he gets bigger, okay?"

He hugged her.

When his eyes grew moist, he realized they'd finally come full circle. He'd gone the distance to protect the sister he loved, and she'd shared the truth with Jolie to protect him.

"So if you need longer to finish things here, can't we just stay and finish?" she suggested, looking back at his numbers. "I heard Uncle Pete say he could handle stuff back home."

"You weren't supposed to be listening," he scolded. "I thought you wanted to get back to your horseback riding lessons."

"Sarah's family has a horse farm not too far away, and her mom said I could come ride with them anytime. And she's like the nicest person I ever met, Pops. I'm just saying it would be all right." Her voice trailed off just enough to leave the thought in his head before she turned and called across the cabin to her little brother. "Sam, wouldn't you like to stay down here for a while? Just to see?"

Sam's uncooperative attitude about homework had cost him screen time, but he'd engrossed himself in creating another card tower at the living room table. One with turrets this time. "I could really love it here if we get to go to those cool places we saw when we were driving around," he called back. "We could at least stay and finish things up, right? Mrs. Smith is really nice and you know that Mrs. P. really doesn't like little boys all that much."

Mrs. P. was the third-grade teacher he'd had in Maryland. Sammy hadn't been a huge fan of hers.

"It might take me several months if I follow through on everything we've started," Shane told them.

"Do you promise it will be pretty when the leaves come back?" Jolie asked in a serious voice, because Jolie was one of those kids who appreciated nature's beauty.

Pretty? How about downright beautiful? He looped

an arm around her shoulders and planted a kiss to her forehead. "It's the Smokies, so, yeah. I can unequivocally state that it's one of the prettiest places on the planet, and you'll get to see that in all its glory real soon."

"Good."

She went back to her side of the table and began tapping on her tablet keys as if their conversation wasn't a big deal.

It was a huge deal.

Shane knew that.

He'd wanted to protect them from the truth, to keep their mother's image pristine, but once again Chrissie had shown just how far she'd come since that fateful day twenty-seven years before. Shane also realized something else he'd wondered about from time to time. If he'd had the decision to make again, after all this time, would he have taken the rap for what happened that day?

Knowing everything he knew now, the answer would be yes. But he was more proud of the fact that he'd made the decision without knowing the outcome. The truth did set folks free. He believed that.

He also believed in second chances, and he'd been willing to give that gift to Chrissie. As Sam pumped a fist in triumph when he finally got that last turret to stand tall and Jolie congratulated him, Shane came to another realization.

Chrissie had given that gift of a second chance right back to him, and that was the best blessing of all.

# Chapter Eighteen

Jess had seen Shane's truck pass by the area twice Monday morning, but with the constant stream of patients, there hadn't been a free moment to cross the road and hunt him down.

It was the kind of busy morning that only underscored the need for good medical help when emergency care was a solid thirty minutes away. Mary had ignored Jess's concerns and come back to work with her. Dee, her mother's office manager, had come in to the temporary clinic office to process insurance claims, and the day had gone smoothly. She was commending Jenny and Dee on a job well done when her phone rang with her normal Monday check-in call from the job recruiter.

Jess lifted her coffee mug and took the call in the back room. "Hey, Courtney."

"I've got news, Jess. Are you sitting down?"

She wasn't, and wasn't about to, but she held the phone tighter. "What's going on?"

"Offers, Jess. Not one, but two. Duke and Cleveland."

Two top facilities reaching out to her.

"I just sent you the emails. Both are eager to chat with you as soon as possible, so video interviews suit them fine. Your résumé speaks for itself, Jess. And they're ready to welcome you by the first of February as their chief emergency room physician."

February first?

That was two weeks away. In two very short weeks, she could be named a physician-in-charge of a major ER. She could reclaim the career she'd planned and worked for. The plan she'd laid out years ago. The fruition of all her dreams.

*Before I knew about Mom.*

She exhaled a breath she didn't know she'd been holding and gave a response she wouldn't have predicted short months ago. "This is wonderful news, but I have to turn them down, Courtney. Can we do that with the utmost respect?"

"Turn them down?" Surprise laced Courtney's voice.

Mary came into the exam room as Jess spoke. She looked at Jess, surprised. And then—

Not so surprised. Concern deepened the furrow between her brows as she caught the gist of the conversation. She crossed the room and laid her hand atop Jess's arm. "I'm not going to let you do this," she began while Courtney was still throwing out questions on the other end of the phone.

Jess took care of Courtney first. "Courtney, go ahead with the refusals, I'll take care of your fee and explain later." She set down her phone and faced her mother head-on. "I'm doing it. And that's that."

Concern shadowed Mary's face. The woman who always sacrificed for others, wasn't accustomed to having the tables turned. "Jess, I—"

"Remember that 'whither thou goest' thing you talk about?" Jess asked calmly. "How you've got it hanging on the office wall, and how your people will be my people?"

"And your God, my God," Mary finished softly.

"Well, I'm staying here and that's that," Jess told her. "I'm not leaving you, Mom. I'm not leaving you in a lurch or this town without a doctor."

"It's a two-person office, Jess. We planned it out that way with Shane so we can sell the practice when we need to. And I'm on borrowed time."

"A reality I understand better than anyone," Jess replied. "You know how it works, Mom. Someone will come along when you're unable to practice and we'll add them on, but for now it's you and me. For as long as God gives us."

"As long as God gives us?" Mary raised her left brow in question as they moved into the front room. Dee and Jenny had gone up the road to the A & M Grocery to grab lunch. "Sweet words coming from my stubborn child's mouth."

Jess swept the clinic a quick look. "I have my share of questions and doubts," she admitted. Then she sighed. "I've never seen the sense in counting on others but when I look at the circumstances that brought us to this point, all the intersections that *had* to happen, I see a plan. And maybe that's God's plan, or maybe it's not, but there's no way it's just a series of coincidences. A smart guy once told me that faith brought him through the worst of the worst. And if that can happen to him, then maybe it's time for a know-it-all like me to pay attention."

"That's where it begins." Mary hugged her tight just as Shane's truck rolled up across the street.

Jess grabbed a coat and tugged her chemo hat down a little tighter. "Just the person I needed to see. I'll be back for our first afternoon patient, all right?"

Mary didn't try to hide her smile of approval. "Very all right."

Jess headed out the door and crossed the road at an angle. She wasn't sure what she'd say to Shane, but she knew exactly how the conversation would begin.

With her apology for sending him to jail.


"I should punch you, Shane Stone."

The sound of Jess's voice—apart from the threat—made him happy, but Shane quelled that reaction before he turned around. "You need a hard hat in here, Jess."

She grabbed one off a sawhorse table and plunked it on her head with such force that he winced. "Easy now."

"My head is fine. My hair may be short but it's no longer nonexistent and it's grayer than I'd like, but I'll deal with that in good time. I came over to say I'm sorry."

Shane exaggerated a look of disbelief intentionally. "By threatening bodily harm?"

"By messing up the life of the most incredible man I know," she whispered, and when he met her gaze…

When his eyes met hers…

He realized she knew. "Jess, you did exactly what you were supposed to do. You—"

"I know what I did." She moved forward until she was right in front of him. A couple of the guys glanced their way, but they were mudding the drywall in the exam rooms and were smart enough to stay there. "I sent an innocent man to prison for a crime he didn't commit, and you let me."

*Yep. She knew, all right.* "I made a choice," he said softly. "The only one I could have made, and if I had to do it again, I'd make the same choice, Jess."

"I know." She reached out. Took his hands. And then she didn't let them go. "And I love you for it. I'm pretty mad at myself right now, that I didn't look beyond what I saw, but when Devlyn told me what happened—"

He winced. "I didn't know that people had figured it out until I came back here. It was a shock."

"You were afraid the kids would find out."

He sighed. "Yes. But I found out last night that Chrissie told Jolie all about it before she died. She wanted her to understand what had happened, and Jolie managed to give me quite the lecture on it last evening. It was a solid wake-up call."

"Out of the mouths of babes." She gripped his hands. "Shane, I'm not saying this to put you on the spot or to mess up your life, but I fell hard for you when I was a teenager and there's a part of me that's never moved beyond that first love."

She said *love.* And not in the past tense.

"I'm staying here." She lifted her chin in a classic Jess stance. "I'm staying here to help Mom and to help the town and the valley. I'm staying here to keep this beautiful doctor's office open, and—"

He kissed her.

He kissed her with great deliberation because he hadn't had a bit of peace since he'd found her teetering on the mountain's edge a month ago. He kissed her because kissing her gave him that sense of fulfillment. A sense he'd been missing for long, long years.

Then he kissed her cheeks, her forehead and her lips again.

His phone chimed a message from Pete.

He ignored it. Right now, there was nothing but Jess Bristol in his thoughts or in his arms. When she finally broke the kiss, he held on, making her lean back to meet his gaze. "You interrupted me with that kiss."

"And you're in danger of being kissed again, so talk fast." He grinned.

"You should probably know I can't have children."

He held her gaze and let her go on.

"I'd already figured out that the whole knight-in-shining-armor thing wasn't going to happen, and I never wanted to be a single parent," she told him. "I was blessed by Mom, but I think having two parents is important. Once we discovered the cancer, it became a non-entity, but I needed to be honest with you because I see how great you are with kids, Shane. And that's something you need to know."

"Is it my turn now?"

She frowned, but he'd grown used to that a long time ago because there was always something on Jess's mind.

He'd consider it an honor to take some of that weight off her very pretty shoulders.

"Fortunately, I have two kids to share."

She started to say something but he put two fingers against her pretty lips to pause her. "My turn."

She made a face but stayed quiet.

"I'm staying here long enough to finish everything. At least through spring, and maybe into summer by the time we get things wrapped up."

"But what about your business in Maryland?"

"Pete will go back north. He'll oversee our projects there, and we're even talking about opening a branch down here."

"In Kendrick Creek?"

"Why not?" He shrugged his shoulders then bracketed her face with his hands. "There's growth happening here, Jess. It's all around us. And what better place to branch out a construction business than in an area like this with the spillover from Gatlinburg and Pigeon Forge and all those retirees coming south?"

"Which means we're both staying." Hope filled her pretty eyes. A hope he'd like to encourage for...oh, say...forever.

"Yes."

She blushed.

Jess never blushed. She wasn't the blushing sort, but when his finger grazed the heat in her cheek, he knew exactly what she was thinking because he was thinking the very same thing.

"We'll have the church ready in a few weeks' time, according to Pete. We'll take down the scaffolds once the final coat of paint is done, and be ready to throw open those windows to welcome spring. There's nothing like a spring wedding in Tennessee, is there? And if there aren't any weddings on the reverend's docket, Jess, I'd be proud to put one on the schedule. If the lady's willing."

She leaned up and kissed him one last time because there were patients due in just a few minutes. "I'd say quite willing, if you're sure, Shane." This time she put her hands along his face. "You've got two kids who already lost their mother. I don't want to scare them. Or worry them. You've already gone through the cancer thing with Chrissie—you know it can be a game changer."

It could. He knew that, but he'd been doing a good share of thinking and praying about this, and a whole lot of other things, too. "If I really trust God, I have to trust Him in all things. Not just the easy stuff. The hard stuff, too. If there's one thing I've learned, it's that second-guessing God is a fruitless act."

"So it seems, because if someone would have laid out this scenario a few months ago, I'd have laughed. But I'm not laughing now." She kissed him one last time and made it a kiss worth remembering. "I think a cozy church wedding with my mother here to give me away would make me outrageously happy, Shane. As long as you're the groom."

He laughed, hugged her close and then stepped back. "Supper, later?"

"Devlyn's making soup."

"I'll bring bread from up the road and two hungry kids. Sound good?"

Her smile filled his heart with a joy he hadn't expected and wasn't sure he deserved, but he was willing to take it. "Sounds perfect."

As she hurried across the street, waving to two patients who were making their way through the chilly damp afternoon, he didn't see the glum dankness or the treetop fog.

It was the beauty of the Blue Ridge that surrounded him. Embraced him. Called him home.

A measure of cold and damp was nothing to a mountain man, but a life with Jess? A life raising kids who needed their faith, love and trust?

Now that was something to call home about.

# Epilogue

The historic small church shone in the mid-March sun. Redbud maples formed ruddy arches against a deep blue sky while daffodils and jonquils added sparks of ground color to gardens, alongside the less welcome henbit and dandelions.

"Jess."

Devlyn was fussing with Jess's headpiece, a tucked satin turban. Jess turned to her mother and smiled. "Please tell me people came."

"The church is full and the charity box is overflowing. You and Shane have such good hearts, Jess. You make me proud."

Contentment filled Jess's heart. More than the medical accolades, her mother's praise and respect was the best award she could ever be given. "I hope I always make you proud, Mama."

Tears filled Mary's eyes.

"Mama, you stop that! Stop that right now!" exclaimed Jess in mock horror, using her full Southern drawl. "We made a promise to one another, and my eye-lashes are thin enough. This fancy mascara is the only thing making them visible!"

Mary laughed.

She took Jess's hands as the sweet bell rang above them. "All right, I did promise. It's just that you made an old woman's—"

Devlyn snorted and Jolie exclaimed, "Doc Mary, you're not old! Why you're hardly older than my dad!"

Mary smiled. "All right, you made a mother's heart feel absolutely wonderful with your strength and grace and faith, Jessica Mary Bristol. And I couldn't be happier than I am today."

"Me, either."

The bell stopped tolling.

It was time to begin the small procession down the vintage church aisle.

Pastor Bob waited at the small sanctuary, and by his side were Shane and Pete, handsome in well-cut suits that neither man was used to wearing. In front of Shane stood Sam, holder of the rings. They'd outfitted the boy in a white button-down shirt with suspenders, and dress pants, a classic country look.

Jolie started down the aisle, sprinkling silk petals along the way.

Devlyn followed. Jed was in the front pew, waiting for his mom and Mary to join him. Sammy and Jolie would sit there, too. A family bound by love.

When Jess stepped through the door on her mother's arm, Shane's look of appreciation was all she saw. He'd showed her so much since that snow-filled rescue.

He didn't dwell on what had been in their pasts. He'd taught her to gaze toward the future God laid out for them. And as she moved down the aisle...

And offered him a teasing smile...

She knew she'd finally come home.

And home was exactly where she wanted to be.

\* \* \* \* \*

*If you loved this story,*
*be sure to pick up Ruth Logan Herne's*
*previous miniseries, Golden Grove*

A Hopeful Harvest
Learning to Trust
Finding Her Christmas Family

*Available now from Love Inspired!*

*Find more great reads at www.LoveInspired.com*

Dear Reader,

I love writing about these midlife heroes and heroines! Remember Frank Capra's *It's a Wonderful Life*, when the curmudgeon calls out George Bailey for not kissing Mary Hatch? "Youth is wasted on the wrong people," he bellows. I laugh every time I hear that because he's right!

I am so blessed to be writing this series, so a huge thank you to my beloved editor, Melissa Endlich, for this vote of confidence. I fall a little more in love with Tennessee on every visit, and if I didn't have eleven grandkids in Western New York, I'd probably find myself in the quiet rolling majesty of the Blue Ridge Mountains. I love it. It suits me! And Shane's sacrifice opened his sister's heart to the light of faith and hope, and she overcame her problems...but made sure he wouldn't pay the price indiscriminately before she died. She came a long way, didn't she?

And Jess was wonderful to write, a female prodigal, only an über-successful one. Jess wasn't digging in pig scraps for food, she was financially sound, but empty inside, exacerbated by illness and unmet goals. But God saw her worth and her future, and it was no accident that brought them together on that hill overlooking Kendrick Creek. And no accident that they saved one another.

Thank you so much for reading this story. I hope you loved it. I love hearing from you guys! Email me at loganherne@gmail.com or friend me on Facebook and/or stop by my website www.ruthloganherne.com. Wishing you bountiful blessings, peace, hope and love!

*Ruthy*

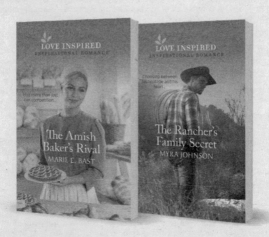

# COMING NEXT MONTH FROM
## Love Inspired

### Available April 27, 2021

## HIDING HER AMISH SECRET
*The Amish of New Hope* • by Carrie Lighte
Arleta Bontrager's convinced no Amish man will marry her after she got a tattoo while on *rumspringa*, so she needs money to get it removed. But taking a job caring for Noah Lehman's sick grandmother means risking losing her heart to a man who has his own secrets. Can they trust each other with the truth?

## TO PROTECT HIS CHILDREN
*Sundown Valley* • by Linda Goodnight
Struggling to find a nanny for his triplets, rancher Wade Trudeau advertises for a housekeeper instead. So when former teacher Kyra Mason applies, looking for a place without children to recover after a tragedy, she's shocked to meet his toddlers. Might this reluctant nanny and heartbroken cowboy find healing together?

## A PLAN FOR HER FUTURE
*The Calhoun Cowboys* • by Lois Richer
Raising his orphaned granddaughter alone seems impossible to Jack Prinz, but he has the perfect solution—a marriage of convenience with his childhood friend. But even as Grace Partridge falls for little Lizzie, convincing her to marry without love might not be so easy...

## THE TEXAN'S TRUTH
*Cowboys of Diamondback Ranch* • by Jolene Navarro
Returning to his family ranch, Bridges Espinoza's surprised to find his cousin's widow—the woman he once secretly loved—there as well. But even more stunning is the boy who arrives claiming to be his son. While the child brings Bridges and Lilianna together, the truth about his parentage could tear them apart...

## THE SHERIFF'S PROMISE
*Thunder Ridge* • by Renee Ryan
After Sheriff Wyatt Holcomb and veterinarian Remy Evans clash over her new petting zoo—and her runaway alpaca!—the two strike a bargain. She'll watch the nephew in his care for the summer if he'll push along the permit process. But keeping things strictly professional is harder than either of them expected.

## SEEKING SANCTUARY
*Widow's Peak Creek* • by Susanne Dietze
When pregnant single mom Paige Latham arrives in Kellan Lambert's bookstore needing a temporary job, he wouldn't dare turn away the sister of his old military buddy. But as they grow closer working together, can they say goodbye before her baby arrives, as planned?

**LOOK FOR THESE AND OTHER LOVE INSPIRED BOOKS WHEREVER BOOKS ARE SOLD, INCLUDING MOST BOOKSTORES, SUPERMARKETS, DISCOUNT STORES AND DRUGSTORES.**

LICNM0421

# Get 4 FREE REWARDS!

## We'll send you 2 FREE Books plus 2 FREE Mystery Gifts.

**Love Inspired** books feature uplifting stories where faith helps guide you through life's challenges and discover the promise of a new beginning.

FREE
Value Over
$20

---

**YES!** Please send me 2 FREE Love Inspired Romance novels and my 2 FREE mystery gifts (gifts are worth about $10 retail). After receiving them, if I don't wish to receive any more books, I can return the shipping statement marked "cancel." If I don't cancel, I will receive 6 brand-new novels every month and be billed just $5.24 each for the regular-print edition or $5.99 each for the larger-print edition in the U.S., or $5.74 each for the regular-print edition or $6.24 each for the larger-print edition in Canada. That's a savings of at least 13% off the cover price. It's quite a bargain! Shipping and handling is just 50¢ per book in the U.S. and $1.25 per book in Canada.* I understand that accepting the 2 free books and gifts places me under no obligation to buy anything. I can always return a shipment and cancel at any time. The free books and gifts are mine to keep no matter what I decide.

Choose one:  ☐ **Love Inspired Romance**
Regular-Print
(105/305 IDN GNWC)

☐ **Love Inspired Romance**
Larger-Print
(122/322 IDN GNWC)

Name (please print)

Address                                                                                          Apt. #

City                                          State/Province                          Zip/Postal Code

**Email:** Please check this box ☐ if you would like to receive newsletters and promotional emails from Harlequin Enterprises ULC and its affiliates. You can unsubscribe anytime.

### Mail to the Harlequin Reader Service:
**IN U.S.A.:** P.O. Box 1341, Buffalo, NY 14240-8531
**IN CANADA:** P.O. Box 603, Fort Erie, Ontario L2A 5X3

Want to try 2 free books from another series! Call 1-800-873-8635 or visit www.ReaderService.com.

---

# LOVE INSPIRED

INSPIRATIONAL ROMANCE

## UPLIFTING STORIES OF FAITH, FORGIVENESS AND HOPE.

---

Join our social communities to connect with other readers who share your love!

Sign up for the Love Inspired newsletter at **LoveInspired.com** to be the first to find out about upcoming titles, special promotions and exclusive content.

---